a

Black Journey: Redemption
The saga of the Morgan family continues

Black Journey: Beginnings
Learn the history of the Nawhe people and their tribal ways.

BLACK JOURNEY

A Novel By: Raymond Davilla

Spirit Walker Press
Albuquerque ♦ New Mexico

Dedication

Dedicated in memory of Helen Wheeler Querdibitty, grandmother and respected elder of the Wichita & Affiliated Tribes of Oklahoma. Helen walked as a true representative of a Christian Native woman, a teacher of our old ways.

Preface

Black Journey was written by the inspiration of God. The overall story was completed in very little time, because He wants the story told. In editing it was revealed the writings have incredible symbolism determining effective life applications with historical and impending relevance.

Black Journey is a fictional adaptation of factual events. Many American Christians are moved by the persecution of Christians abroad, unaware of similar consequences on their own soil.

Additionally, Christianity is on the decline, because of the lack of taking a stand and a desire to quench it.

Every person must make a decision or continue the Black Journey.

Introduction

Every Native people is steeped in a rich history of cultural practices. This composition declares their identity. Identity is the thread of character which defines the people's nature. Who you are can be based upon thousands of years of history or yesterday's adoption. Either way, your identity can develop to historical maturity or be transformed by creative or violent influence. Native Americans of every sort have been transformed by a variety of influential factors. Most have been physical efforts; however there is much that remains in the makeup of Native people touched by mystical spiritual influences. From long ago to the present age, the Native people are still defined by mystical ways that intrigue outsiders.

Language, art, music, beliefs, and other social customs are remarkable keys to the character and history of all Native people and nations.

There are ties to the people's survival by various customs; art records language and beliefs; and through music, beliefs are sustained. Through education and rearing, refinement fosters survival.

Music encourages dance which exhibits laughter, celebration and courage. Survival takes many forms; mere existence, existence in perfection and everything in between.

Among Native people survival takes on another myriad of possibilities. Survival in its capacity of mere existence is easily imaginable. But move up the chain of preferences and survival or life turns that corner of grandeur.

The realm of all social and religious events lies within the foundation to define the people as a people. The age in which they live prepares the people for progress. Their next trial is opportunity for escalation of self-reliance. But trials to Natives haven't always proven to be an opportunity of self-reliance. Instead, adversity has created a necessity of interdependence.

The previous trials refine the counteractions of future outcome. As time moves forward and influences begin to impact the culture, survival begins to take on a new image. A tribe often times seeks to preserve its culture at the sacrifice of some of the other social elements, while strengthening those things most important.

What is most important? Language, art, beliefs? What is the true priority of the people? Can all things remain intact that gave credence to their identity? Can all things remain intact even while the world begins to infringe upon their perfect realm of life?

Can a people improve on their lives, from a point they once thought as perfect or will they or outsiders destroy themselves from any identity at all? Our Native people have faced this tale of constant change since their inception to this world.

Every Native people is different, and obviously change has come and will continue to impact the first Americans until life has reached a point of stability and then change again. Minor or major, good or bad, change is only as important as its benefits, and one's convictions.

Amazingly Native America has experienced a lot more than just being the object of conquest. Which is more than the outside world would either care to imagine or give credence of occurrence.

This aboriginal people have an inconceivable responsibility to burden a link to a forgotten world. When the European subjugators relished their prize of the Americas, they belittled its occupants.

Savages, barbarians, uncivilized creatures; "these people must be tempered from their gross neglect of culture and refinement."

These so called savages in fact originated as conveyors of a crucial unknown link to their vanquishers. Any link to these people was never considered laudable. After all, where did these people come from? Even today their link is trivial.

Historical studies only further confuse the greatest scholarly minds. Where is the link? Why aren't there any clear chronicles of these peoples? Why do their abstract annals only confuse the learned and seem to either be dead ends or meaningless hieroglyphics? Grand assumptions cannot begin to quench the actual oceanic thirst of consideration pertinent to meet the true revelation of the Natives' origins.

Close open investigation affords a pyramid of astonishment and wonder. Life has greater meaning than many allow. Even the most educated limit their understanding, because of preconceived knowledge.

After all what is knowledge; but a learned limit? Faith, however, is phrased as "the substance of things hoped for and the evidence of things not seen." For the knowledged to become more knowledgeable they must move beyond their limits. Are the blind incapable of discernment because they are limited by their lack of visual sight; or are they afforded greater options of perception?

This story is an old lesson in growth. The people must learn to listen with their hearts, while their conqueror must learn to be educated. Both have limits that destroy potential progress. Distractions from truth and social growth hinders monumental strides for advancement. In all that is done, if distractions took on an obvious appearance, fewer opportunities would be missed.

This story is more than a story, and not just a lesson, because perception goes beyond appearances. In all that you hear and see, comprehend the truth.

Chapter One

The Invitation

In the southwestern desert land there is a people who knew the earth from the time when life was simple, stability was rock solid. The spirit beings that gave them instruction led them in survival. This instruction meant survival in battle with enemies of man, elements and spirits. They adapted to the harshness of their climate that would rob them of harvest and life.

1

They adapted to the greed of other tribes that sought their possessions, food, land and lives. They stood against the white man when he desired all they had.

Great destruction came upon every Native tribe. The Native people won few battles and lost many. How do you fight an enemy whose god is great and the people don't fight fair? A treaty here, sacrificed land and lives there, but now peace, peace and new ways. A people are renowned by their culture when they achieve refinement or superiority or keep the truths of their culture's points secret from the outside world, after all this practice would spare their identity.

In the desert southwest the winter can be harsh; when you are not prepared, it can be devastating. When the skies are clear at night the heat of the day is released into the heavens causing a bitter cold that can chill the soul of a man.

In the cold desert night a circular framed mud and stone structure allows a shifting stream of smoke to release from its crudely fashioned chimney and spiral up into the black crisp night air. The smoke lofts eastward to an ever so gentle night current. A window, about the size of a man's head, sparkles brightly as the sole source of light for miles around.

In the doorway there is only a heavy blanket keeping out the cold winter night's air. The strong words of argument seep through the thick wool blanket from the dwellers inside. History is being written this night, the commencement of a spark of growth of a people.

"I tell you, it will be a good thing if they build this house. They promise food in these hard times, clothing and blankets in these cold months. They will bring good medicine for our sick. How can these things be evil? The government isn't keeping their promises. We must accept this hand extended in a good way!" Desertwind, the youngest of the councilmen pleads.

The other councilmen sitting on the cold dirt floor nod in agreement and a few release a low growl of "yeah" in their Nawhe language.

"You are wrong my brother. They come bearing gifts with one hand and carry a knife to strike us down with the other!" yells Johnny Darkeyes, the older war chief.

"You don't see what I see. They want to cut our hair and change our tongue. They want to make our children as stiff boards in their schools, and kill the spirit beings! How is this a good way?"

3

The experienced warrior sitting with a stiff back and great emotion with deep resolve in his voice causes more of the men to begin to take his side.

"My woman is sick, she will die soon. Nauchee, the great medicine man, can do nothing. The white man says they have medicine and medicine men who can heal her. It is nothing for them. I am willing to cut my hair if it means my woman lives!" Desertwind reasons.

"Yes, but I would let my woman die if it means they could not kill our spirits!" Darkeyes brazenly defends, "Our spirits are angry we even consider the white man's words. We must put up our heart's shield against their ways!"

"Does it mean our people will become ignorant of our ways, because the white men build a house!?" Desertwind interjects, "We must look at the benefits to our people. Our elders and children are our richest treasures. If we slap this open hand we cut our treasures' throats. We must have mercy on our own people!"

"I have heard stories of the white men destroying other Native people. They bring their ways and make the Natives as women without hearts! We have learned from our history; sometimes there must be a sacrifice. The elders know what it means to be weak and hold our people back. The children are stronger than you think. If they are not strong perhaps it would be best if they did not survive!" Darkeyes argues.

Desertwind points his finger at Darkeyes across the crowded room filled with smoke from the tobacco pipe.

"Look here Darkeyes, I care for my woman and if I have to be a slave to the white man so she can live, then bring me the chains!" Desertwind passionately exclaims.

"You are a coward for your woman, Desertwind" Darkeyes snarls, "Our spiritual ways must live. They have carried us for generations. If we give in to their ways we will become as a wolf without a coat. We will shiver in the cold, like a sickly old woman!"

The Grand Elder, Mountainhawk raises his hand. The younger men immediately hush from their argument, their facial expressions still filled with conflict.

The room filled with two dozen of the village elders and councilmen, turn their heads to listen to the chief. Usually the company of tribesmen sits down to discuss their concerns, but this was no usual subject. The old man rises to his feet. His feeble legs shake then steady to support his old tired frame. The crowd watches him rise, and the two on either side reach their hands out to support him. Slowly rising, he gestures, waving his hand he doesn't need any help.

The frail elder begins to look around the room into each set of eyes, as he is arched as a worn bow. He begins to look around the room adorned with many relics of past battles and dancing regalia, clubs, staffs, bows and quivers, shields and spears, beautiful colored leggings and breast plates, racks of deer and elk.

He breaths deeply the aroma of pipe smoke that is mingled with the fragrance of burning incense of sage and the musk of the men and the staleness of hides of every kind of animal, that now fill his lungs and his sense of smell causes his memories to revisit better times.

It is a place of esteem among the men, their history is here, and their future looms by his words. The old man takes it all in with a glisten of accomplishment in his eyes.

He clears his throat several times, showing the stress of age and the night air upon his old body. Finally in a clear tone the elder councilman begins to slowly speak.

"We have come together to speak of this white man's house on our land… many have argued while we smoke the pipe. Brother against brother, our eyes are dim like an old man before his last journey. All of you have spoken well… which way do we turn our hearts? I have listened to the hard words for and against this white man's house for many days.

It is hard to let outsiders come in when they don't know our ways and they seek to change our people. Are these white men our enemy? Do they want harm to come upon our heads? I have fought against many enemies… from the time when I was a boy… until not many years ago. But Desertwind is right," He pauses to moisten his lips, biting his lip and tongue together. "We don't have enough strength to feed ourselves and fight off the sicknesses that kill our people. This reservation land has given up much of the life we once relied on to survive. The spirits have taken away the rich soil and have slowed the waters and caused the animals to move north out of the boundaries set by the white man.

These white men have a strong spirit teaching them. They have medicine men who can heal our people at death's sunset, while our shaman looks dazed as a newborn child against these sicknesses.

7

We have never argued against those of strong medicine.

Is it good to fall to your death hanging from a cliff with your last ounce of strength? Or is it better to take the outstretched hand of your enemy and live to fight another day? It's as Desertwind says, our people are strong in our ways, and we won't let them forget, because the white man builds his house." The elder tribal leader's eyes narrow and he looks intently at his audience, "Our children are our children..." pointing his thumb at the middle of his chest. "We still have their ears, just because they sit in the white man's schoolhouse doesn't mean they stop being Nawhe...."

Many of the men nod in agreement and voice their approval of his comments. Darkeyes grows uncomfortable as he snorts in disgust.

"If they will feed us and clothe us and heal our sick then let them build this house, we will still be Nawhe!" confirms Mountainhawk.

After his words the room is filled with many gestures of agreement, except for Darkeyes, who shakes his head in disagreement.

"Go tell the white men they can build this medicine lodge" instructs Mountainhawk.

Desertwind says, "I will go and tell them, but they wants us to know this house is not a medicine lodge."

"Then what is the name of this house they want to build, Desertwind?" Mountainhawk asks.

"They call it Church." Desertwind replies.

"Go, take word to these white men and tell them they can build their Church" Mountainhawk affirms.

Word is taken to the white men and they receive it with great joy as an enormous battle has been won. The white men organize themselves and bring many wagon loads of building supplies. They bring a crew of many carpenters to build their church.

After a short while a church begins to take shape from its strong cornerstones for its foundation to the tall framed walls and pitched roof. A beautiful church with white walls and colorful glass windows. A shiny slick glazed wood floor and strong wooden pews line the sanctuary and a broad maple pulpit takes center stage. The church can be seen from all over the village on the valley floor. Its tall steeple is adorned with a white cross on the very top. It stands as a flag placed over a battlefield for a marker of victory.

The Nawhe watch daily at the progress of the structure. They whisper to one another, "Is this a small fort?" and "Are we welcome in such a place?"

Soon the church is completed and they find out all its purposes. The church fulfills its promises and brings food, medicine and clothing.

The Nawhe accept these gestures of harmony and survival. The tribe begins to flourish, disease is all but defeated.

Joy comes to the desert village. Prosperity seems to be dawning on the distant horizon. But they soon realize the focal intent of the church, to teach them a new belief.

The people keep their promises to one another and hold on to their Nawhe ways. The people sit in the beautiful house of worship, but it is only a token gesture. The people are in one accord, to withstand any words of conversion to this white man's God; their hearts are black as the midnight hour.

The years go by and the church begins to age. Time goes by and few visitors pass her doors. The support from the outsiders dwindles, very little food, not even enough for a full meal, no medicine, no blankets and faded, worn clothes from another age.

Another year, another decade goes by and the church shows her age all the more. She is as a pandemic of difficult years has taken her down from her once model of beauty. No one cares, not enough to bring her back now from the brink of decay. Where are those who promised her message? Where are those who had compassion for a hurting people?

No, the work is too hard, the message misunderstood. Let her perish, there isn't a need, by the recipients' own hands. In her youth the little white church saw her share of miracles. There were those who came to receive medicine, but received healing by the white preacher's prayers instead.

Illnesses that placed their possessor at death's threshold came back with new life. Sicknesses that turned practical corpses into youthful beings vanished with simple faith and prayers of a compassionate pastor. Those consumed with alcohol, the tribe had banished as outcasts, now were rightful members of respect.

Certain ones of the Nawhe gave the white man's God a chance. Their hearts were reborn, their lives turned around, but the Nawhe had a pact, no one would ever receive the white man's God. The Nawhe refused to relinquish their spiritual ways and instead rejected the white man's gospel.

Still, there were a few who could not defy the drawing of the mystical phenomenon. The white man's God was strong and could not be denied.

And so it began... a long saga of killing their own whom refused to abandon the white man's God. It was a clandestine practice that unsettled the village.

So early in her infancy the sparkling structure of great hope now lies as a symbol of death and fear. So the inevitable demise of her beauty waits.

The church's pastors change like the seasons of the desert valley. This pastor has a strong will and desires service to his God and potential congregation, but his will and desire are both broken by lack of finances, the passage of time with no followers, and the death of his only saved soul in two years.

A mutilated corpse is discovered on the church steps one winter morning. It could only be assumed to be that of the missing newborn Christian.

The spring comes with new life for the desert flowers and a new pastor who will fall victim to the coming failures.

His heart and will aren't as strong as the last's. He's only there as a stepping stone to better assignments with better wages and congregation.

"These heathen are like the savages of old, they don't know what's good for them, serving devils and smoke!" criticizes the pastor.

So with no effort, no spirit and no hope the now broken pastor moves on only after a little while. The little white church sees years of neglect and locked doors, but soon there would be another gospel proclaiming minister and another. Some come with grand ideas; a revival, a set of puppets, a handout of Christmas sacks.

But no screaming preacher, no puff of material with button eyes, no brown paper bag with goodies of candy and oranges could sway the hardened Nawhe to accept the good news that was proclaimed for decades.

So the saga continues…

Chapter Two

Purity of Innocence

A beautiful early fall evening begins in the quiet desert southwest. An Indian reservation town of Banshee wafts below the billowing approaching storm clouds, which overtake the brilliant blue skies that have dominated the day.

The small community is dotted with scant, shabby houses in front of a backdrop of distant mesas. The mesas, a Spanish word for table tops, appear just as the meaning.

The bright and dark orange, red, tan and brown shaded landscaped table tops add magnificent color and glamour to the otherwise drab village of Banshee.

The community is strategically situated in a serene location from the rest of the world, a place rarely affected by outside influence. The clouds rise ever more heavenly and even closer to the village below. The heat of the day greets an evening storm and begins to shape scenes of foretelling over the town.

The modern day Indian dwellers find peace before the storm. But one home unknowingly prepares for a storm of the century. The echoes of powerful argument rise above the evening air, more powerful than the cloud burst over the mesas.

"I told you woman, there's no way that yer gonna bring that nonsense in this house, no day, no way!" yells a strong determined masculine Native voice.

"Ben, I told you, this is my home too, and I'm not living if I can't have joy in my own home!" the woman proclaims.

"Julie, I just got ya that new crock pot like you been wantin'. Ya said that's all you wanted for your birthday, and now ya want to bring a bunch of nosey old biddies in here, preaching all that nonsense?!" gripes Ben.

"You've been eatin' awfully good since we got that crock pot, and I'm not just talking mutton stew. And you know those women just want to get together to study a little of God's Word." Julie tries to diplomatically assure.

"Woman, if I told you once, I've told you a hundred times, that Jesus crap is gonna get you killed! There's people in the village that have heard what yer tryin' to do.

We've tried to keep that junk from destroying our lives and culture like it's done to so many other Native people and communities.

They say they're about love, hell, they've killed a whole lot more Indians than they ever loved!

The villagers are already makin' threats. You know what happened to the Wheelers two years ago.

Nobody even questioned what happened, they just buried them. There are elders and leaders that run everything, and Christianity isn't a part of this community, it's not Nawhe.

I'm still surprised that church ever got built in the village. It should have got burned down years ago.

Some claim there are strong spirits protecting it, and that has intimidated anyone from doing anything to it or the pastor."

"Ben, I know you're concerned, I'm not doing it because I'm trying to shame you. I'm doing it because the Lord told me to. You believe your ways and I believe mine. You said you respected me for it." Julie defends.

"I said I respected you for having your faith. I know that the Jesus Spirit is very strong with you, ever since you were a little girl.

Your mother's influence even from the grave caused you to follow the white man's religion that she accepted before you were born.

But before, it wasn't affecting the village, and now you're talking about taking some of the wives and convertin' them to Christianity.

They aren't going to stand for it. I'm tellin' ya, they aren't going to stand by and let it happen. We've been having this same argument for two years now.

Please listen to me honey, please, what else can I say to you that will change your mind?" Ben begs.

"I know what you're saying" Julie whispers, "but I have to obey my Lord, not those who don't understand Him.

He spoke to me very clearly, it's His plan. I can't argue with Him, you understand, don't you Ben?"

"Even if it means your life Julie?" Ben cries.

"Even if it means my life, honey, even if it means my life!" Julie sternly confirms.

"What if we lose you? We'll be lost!"

"They're all lost, if I don't try!" Julie exclaims.

"Okay, Babes, I won't argue with you about it anymore. I know you're gonna do it no matter what. You can have your Bible studies here once a month, but like I said before, the boys aren't to be a part of it, alright?" Ben determines.

"Alright, the boys can stay away that night, I promise." Julie concedes.

"You're just a big ol' softee, no matter how hard a front you try to put up" Julie gleefully professes.

The two hug and kiss, and lay their heads on one another's shoulders. Julie cries with tears of joy, while Ben sheds tears of anguish.

The snow is deep on a bright sunny day, two white rabbits forage for a morsel of winter grass beneath the frozen blanket of snow. The rabbits become frantic as the air is filled with the scent of danger.

The fear rises and they bounce off one another in anticipation of the obvious onslaught.

And to the confirmation of their senses three scruffy coyotes dart from the forest trees toward the frighten rabbits.

The rabbits dash off in the opposite direction from their pursuers, but their plight last only a short while.

They are overtaken and quickly killed without mercy by their hungry assailants.

The coyotes rip the rabbits apart, spewing blood across the white snow.

One of the coyotes snatches the carcasses from the other two as if claiming a trophy.

"Daniel, Daniel! Daniel, get up sleepy head, you boys come and eat!" Julie's voice calls.

Daniel's face shows fright as the call breaks the nightmare's hold of his spirit.

"What, what? I'm up, okay, I'm coming." Daniel wearily affirms, still shaken by the rabbits' encounter.

The teenage boy throws the blanket from his body, stretches and rolls himself out of his bed.

"Get up shrimp." he exclaims to his little brother still asleep across the room.

"Huh…?" the little boy moans.

Daniel grabs the blankets and jerks them off his brother, leaving the little boy exposed in his underwear, quickly curling into the fetal position to protect himself from the cool morning air.

"Jerk!" the sibling growls.

Daniel laughs in ridicule. He then staggers down the hall toward the bathroom.

The door closes as he practices his morning ritual of preparation for the day.

Within a short time Daniel appears from the bathroom groomed and refreshed for all the day has to offer.

He tucks into his room to find his little brother absent from his bed.

Daniel completes his preparation by pulling out a tee shirt from a dresser drawer. He quickly dresses and makes his way toward the delicious aromas of breakfast lofting throughout the house.

"Mmm smells good Ma" Daniel compliments as he kisses his mother good morning and begins to dig in.

"Jordan didn't even brush his teeth Ma." Daniel tells on his little brother.

"So?" Jordan defends.

"Yeah, so?" Becky, his old sister replies, hugging her little brother like a mother bear. "You used to eat worms when you were Jordy's age, I haven't seen him do that!"

"Ewww, gross, Danny ate worms!" Jordan disgustingly remarks, holding his little hand to his mouth.

"Okay, okay, you haven't got long to eat. You're gonna be late for school if you don't hurry." Julie scolds.

"I don't know why you wouldn't get up. I've been hollering at 'cha for twenty minutes."

"Sorry Ma. I was into a pretty intense dream, it really had a hold on me, it scared me. The last thing I was thinking about was getting up for school." Daniel explained.

"Yeah speaking of which I gotta go, see everybody after school, bye Jordy, by Mom, see ya worm boy!" Becky calls, darting out the front door.

"Worm boy, yer gonna find a bunch of worms in yer hair in the morning!" Daniel threatens.

"Hey cut it out Daniel Jameson Morgan! That is no way for a teenager to behave." corrects Julie.

"Sorry Ma. She just burns my cookies, treatin' me like she so much older."

"Anyway Daniel, tell me about your dream." Julie requests.

"Oh yeah, I was having a dream and it seemed so real, it had a grip on me, it really upset me." Daniel confesses.

"Sorry honey, what was the dream about?" Julie inquires.

"Aw nothing just about some rabbits gettin' chased and eatun' by some coyotes. It really upset me though, those coyotes didn't have any mercy on those rabbits at all. I'm surprised it bothered me that much. Dad and I go huntin' rabbits all the time. It's just a part of the circle of life to eat animals to survive. We still respect the life that they give up like Dad says." Daniel informs.

"Well you know Daniel, a lotta times dreams have a much greater meaning than just what's being shown to you, it's like I said before, I think God is giving you a special gift. Your dream may mean much more. He'll tell you in time what it means.

It's just like among our people the coyote is a symbol for death and rabbits are a symbol of innocence. Sometimes the innocent die, like you said it's just a part of life." Julie explains.

"Yeah I know, but for some reason it just really hurt that those rabbit's died" Daniel reaffirms, "This one coyote ripped what was left of the rabbits from the other two, like it was his idea to eat them in the first place, it was weird. Anyway on a different subject I heard you and Dad arguing about your Bible study again."

"Well did you hear the finale?" Julie asks

"No, the usual I'm sure, he said NO." Daniel replies.

"No, as a matter of fact he said yes!" Julie gleefully informs.

"Really Mom? That's cool. I'm glad you finally get to do it, but the way Dad tells it, it could mean some serious trouble." Daniel warns.

"Don't worry Honey, your Dad's just a worry wart. It's just a Bible study, no big deal, it's not like we're killing anyone." Julie jokes.

"Well I've heard rumors around the village that they don't want any Christian practices to replace our Nawhe ways, sounded pretty serious to me. They are talking about it like it some great threat."

"It's just a few ladies from church, with me and Becky and maybe we'll invite others as time goes along. Your Dad said its OK, but you and Jordan can't come." Julie shares.

"Well I'm glad to hear that! That stuff is boring, I've got enough religion with the ceremonies." Daniel says, "and enough studying from school."

"Now Daniel you know I've taught you an awful lot about the Lord and His word and the Nawhe ceremonies aren't good." Julie insists, "you've seen those spirits, they're just up to no good!"

"I know, but you know how Dad feels, he... hey I'm gonna be late for school, better go. I'll see ya later Ma." Daniel promises, as he grabs a tortilla and wraps it around some bacon then dashes out the door.

The school bell rings as Daniel races down the dusty dirt road.

He can see in the distance the children quickly entering the small white school building as if they're stuck in a great vacuum.

"Hurry, hurry!" Daniel quietly says to himself, in a fast stride.

He reaches the school and leaps the porch steps, rockets inside and rushes down the hall.

He glances in the small classroom to see if he can sneak past the teacher's inspection.

Daniel has a smile of hope as the teacher writes on the chalkboard. He slowly opens the door as the attentive students quietly tease at his late arrival.

Dan jerks his finger to his lips and throws it downward in a gesture of "sshhh."

He takes his seat with a low creak of his chair. He grimaces in fear of the inevitable, as some of the female students place their hands over their mouths.

"Daniel, if we were watching a mystery movie, you would already have missed the coming attractions, the opening credits and the who done it." quips the old teacher.

"Sorry Mrs. Humphrey." Daniel apologizes.

"Daniel I told you, if you were late one more time, you were going to clean the girl's restroom." Mrs. Humphrey reminds. "Well young man, see the janitor for the mop!"

Daniel slumps in his chair as the other children laugh him to scorn.

"Aw come on Mrs. Humphrey!" Daniel pleads.

"Late is late Daniel, and don't forget to scrub the toilets!" she taunts.

The class bursts out in ridicule, Daniel shakes his head in disgust. He rises from his chair and heads out the classroom door.

Later that day Daniel sits down to lunch with his best friend Carl. "Oh man she ripped you bad, Dan-O... missed the coming attractions..." Carl scoffs.

"Just shut up, I wasn't even 5 minutes late!" Daniel defends.

"Late is late Daniel, and what's that fresh pine smell?" Carl jokes with a sniff of the air.

"Carl one more word and I'm telling how you wear yer Momma's panties when you don't have any clean underwear!" Daniel threatens.

"OK, OK, Danny Boy, I was just kiddin'." Carl assures. "Ya know yer just a little too serious nowadays."

"Well we're growing up, besides I'm worried about Mom. I think she might be gettin' in to some serious stuff." Daniel informs.

"What do ya mean, like drugs?" Carl wonders.

"No, not drugs, ya loon. She told me this mornin' Dad agreed to let her have her Bible Study at the house."

"What? The Bible Study? I told ya Dad said if she starts that stuff, there's gonna be real hell to pay!" Carl remarks, "He says it'll kill our Nawhe ways!"

"I know, I know, that's why I'm worried. This place hates Christians. Mom hasn't been able to speak to half of the women in the village because of it."

"Yeah I know. My Mom likes yer Mom, but Dad said he doesn't ever want to see her talking with yours. The only reason I can talk to you is cause of the ceremonies." Carl fearfully comments, contemplating the loss of his best friend. "Dad says it's like a plague. Ya have ta kill it before it kills you."

"Come on, it's not that bad. Ma's told me a lot of stuff about the Christian way and there's nothing wrong with it." Daniel explains.

"See that? You're already converted!" Carl fears.

"No I'm not. I don't believe in that stuff. You know I accept our ways. It might be scary, but it's the Nawhe way!" Daniel declares.

"Speakin' of ceremonies are ya going Friday night?" Carl asks.

"Of course I am, ya dope, why wouldn't I?" Daniel questions.

"Well I just figured being a Christian an' all, you'd have second thoughts." Carl jokes.

"Hey man, I'm having trouble enough as it is. I don't need that kinda hassle too!" Daniel gripes.

"Yeah, you don't want to clean the restrooms at the ceremonies, or bushes I mean." Carl harasses.

The school bells rings.

"Dude, you were saved by the bell, cause I was gonna tell about your panties!" Daniel warns.

"Yeah, yeah." Carl worries. The two argue all the way back to class.

***

The smell of fried chicken encompasses the little house as Ben springs on to the porch and pulls the screen door open.

"Wow, now that smells like some serious fried chicken, and can it be ... Julie's famous fry bread? Mmmmm.... Fry bread so light the clouds get jealous!" Ben compliments.

"And fried chicken. See, give me what I want and I'll give you what you want." Julie pledges.

"You know I can't stop worrying about it. It's like our whole lives are gonna be changed." Ben speculates.

"Please Babes, please keep it quiet about the Bible study, alright?"

"Sure, we'll be quiet as church mice!" Julie laughs. "Get cleaned up and tell the kids to come on, let's eat!"

"Hey you kids come and eat!" Dad yells as he washes up at the kitchen sink. He dries his hands on a kitchen towel and grabs Julie around her waist from behind as she finishes setting the dinner table.

Ben pulls her to his body and kisses her below the ear.

"Hey Casanova, the kids are coming." Julie warns.

"Yeah? Let'm get their own gal!" Ben defies.

"Alright guys, little ones are present..." Becky informs, as the trio crash the room at once.

"Yeah, little ones like me!" Jordan pipes.

"Ain't nothing we haven't seen on TV." Daniel proclaims.

"Isn't anything, and you need to be careful what you're watching on TV, young man." Julie corrects, as they all sit down at dinner table.

"Just kidding Ma." Daniel backtracks. "Boy, smells delicious Ma, fried chicken, fry bread and squash-corn stew! This is livin', what's the occasion?" Daniel inquires.

"Oh just celebrating your Daddy being an agreeable fellow is all." Julie glistens, winking at Ben.

"What does that mean?" Daniel asks.

"It's grownup talk Dum Dum, means none of ya bizness!" Jordan remarks.

"No, it's just thanking your father for being a loving husband, is all." Julie informs.

"Thanks Dad." Becky gleefully sings.

"Yeah Dad, thanks, you should do it more often." Daniel encourages.

"Alright, alright are we gonna eat this feast or are we gonna give thanks all night?" Ben asks.

"Yeah we gotta give thanks." Jordan reminds.

"Okay, how about you Jordan, you give thanks tonight." Julie requests.

"Ya mean to Daddy or God?" Jordan asks.

"What about Conga?" Ben asks, looking cross at Julie.

"Well how about Jordan thank the Lord tonight." Julie requests, humbly glancing back at Ben.

"Okay." Jordan agrees. "Lord we thank you for some really good smelling chicken and fry bread, I really don't want any squash stew, bless our bodies, amen."

"Amen" the family says in unison.

Chapter Three

Two Sparrows Fall

The blackness of the still summer night is illuminated by the moonlight upon the desert floor. The nocturnal insects and animals fill the air with a harmony of pleasant relaxing melody.

The village rests in the late night tranquility of her habitat. There in the midst of her serenity is the dull thud of mournful labor in the village cemetery.

All that can be seen is a hand grasping a two-foot tall cross crudely made out of old scrap lumber. In the other hand is a hammer striking the top of the cross, as it is slowly driven into the dry desert ground.

A cross in this place. This was the final resting place of Nawhe warriors and former spiritual leaders, the brotherhood of past shaman.

This cemetery saw many ceremonies of pomp and circumstance of the Nawhe burial rituals.

Blood and smoke, feathers and knives.

But tonight this place is the place of Christian reverence, shielded from Nawhe consequence. At every strike of the hammer; memories show scenes of quaking moments leading to this point. The scenes are that of two Native women walking along a dark dirt road. They are in a quick pace, panic is revealed upon their faces.

They turn their heads in quick jerking motions towards the rear, they see they are being pursued. Someone is after them that strikes great fear in their hearts. This fear is reflected in their eyes.

They glance at one another in desperation as they pant to keep their pace. It is Julie and Becky.

"Run baby!" Julie calls.

Becky cries. "Momma!"

The ladies find it difficult to run in their long skirts and dressy shoes. Just then the mother loses one of her shoes, she stumbles as her daughter grasps her arm to keep her upright. The mother tries to run without the one shoe on, knowing there's no time to remove it and start running again.

"Go on Becky!" she cries, "Go on!"

"I'm not leaving you Momma!" Becky cries in determination.

A figure catches their eyes as they look to the opposite side of the road and see a figure of a man standing beside a tall bush and then at a second glance a wolf appears in the same spot.

Each additional flash back to the sound and scene of the hammering cross reveals the women being over taken by their pursuers and the frightful shoving and beating with clubs by several large brutish Native men covered in furs and war paint.

The women are mercilessly beaten, blood spews across the road. The screams give way to the silence of night once more, with the lingering thudding sound of the clubs.

As the scene flashes back and forth between the two scenes of the cemetery and the attack, the scene in the cemetery reveals a dark figure kneeling almost against the small cross.

After a few blows of the hammer, the moonlight reflects off his hands and chest as he reaches in his shirt to reveal a silver crucifix attached to a chain.

He stretches the chain and crucifix over the top of the wooden crosses and begins to slowly wave the pendant in a circular motion several times over the grave makers and draws it to his lips kisses it and places it back in his shirt.

He quotes in a stern rich voice, "Blessed are the pure in heart for they shall see God."

The dark figure stands up and bows his head in respect to the two freshly marked graves.

***

A bright blue daylight fills the sky. Suddenly there is the blast of a loud ringing school bell and gleeful screaming of children as they are being released from school at day's end.

A few high puffy white clouds look down from the beautiful deep blue sky upon the kids running and jumping off a set of concrete steps in front of a small tattered school building. The Native children burst from the doors and rush in all directions to their home destinations.

The thin teenage shabbily dressed Daniel comes pouncing out the door and down the steps. His moppy black hair bounces in time to his giant steps off the school portal.

His worn pale blue tee shirt two sizes too small reads, "Custer's Last Stand" in large bold print and beneath it in small type says, "You want fries with that?" He turns to confirm his hefty schoolmate Carl is close behind.

Daniel argues, "I don't care what you say, that "D" isn't gonna stop me from gett'n to college some day."

"Ur kidding ur self, Dan, if ya think Old Lady Sims is gonna let ya pass her English class!" Carl quips.

As Dan pauses for a moment he glances at a church across the street from the school, his face turns to that of anger and remorse.

"Nope" Carl continues, "you can kiss college goodbye. Yer stuck here with the rest of us dumb ndans."

"It was just a short essay." Dan replies, "I wasn't even tryin'. It was a hurry up thing, cause I had to cook last night."

"Oh yeah." Carl respectfully responds, with a slow backward jerk of his head.

As they have been walking down the dirt road away from the school, Dan hears the sound of a jet plane.

He stops in his tracks and looks up, his wondering eyes fix on a plane high in the sky.

"Ya see that, Carl? One day I'm gonna be up there flying back and forth all across this country and maybe around the world being a famous reporter!" Dan proclaims with pride in his eyes.

"Yeah right, not gettin "D's" in no English class!" Carl snaps. They continue their walk.

"What do ya want to be up there for? If Creator wanted us to fly like eagles He would have given us wings!" Carl sternly suggests, "Or at least a good jet pack." he says with a low chuckle.

Abruptly Dan stops causing dust to fly at his worn tennis shoes.

As he looks to the side of the road and stares at the ground, he immediately sees the flash backs of the two women being beaten.

He hears the screams of "No!" and "Jesus!" as a book falls to the ground in the flash back it hits the ground at the same time Dan's school book hits the ground at his feet startling him and bringing him out of his trance of the images.

Carl stops walking, realizing Dan isn't with him anymore.

He turns back as Dan is coming out of his trance. As he looks at Dan with compassion and pity he states, "Man I wish there was another way to walk home."

"Yeah me too" sniffs Dan, "Me too. Hey man I've gotta get home quick and start cooking some mutton or there's not gonna be any supper!"

"Yeah, nuttin' but muttin'" Carl remarks jokingly, "I get tired of muttin, wish I had me a big ol' steak!"

"You eat your air steak, I've gotta cook some muttin!" Dan yells as he runs down the dirt road, causing a dust cloud behind him.

"See ya tomorrow Steak Hunter!" Dan calls.

"Steak Hunter." Carl grumbles.

After a short sprint, Dan approaches an old bar with worn unpainted walls and a deep shaded porch. As he runs past he glances at several men sitting on the porch staring at him.

Their stares are that of seriousness and determination. One of men's eyes narrows on Dan, and then he grits his teeth in disgust.

The three men assume their positions as lords of the manor. One of the onlookers stands and takes an authoritative position with his tall muscular frame.

He takes a quick drink from his beer bottle and then throws it skidding across the dirt road. Dan hurdles his long legs over the approaching bottle.

The lanky awkward figure of the second man laughs a goofy laugh and encourages, "Good shot Poncho!"

Dan's jaw tightens as he looks dead in the eyes of Poncho and then quickly glances at the third man, a bulky chaste looking character.

The hefty man lightly shakes his head in disapproval at the throw.

Dan looks away and continues to run. After another 10 minutes Dan's running shoes hit the wooden slate porch of his raggedy old home.

He grabs the handle of the screen door and heads inside. He sees his younger brother watching cartoons in the small living area.

The windows are open to let the fresh air in the musty old house to cool it from the rising heat.

"Dad's not home yet?" Dan asks, setting his school book down.

"Nope, good thing for you." his brother quips, "better git supper goin'."

"I know Tumbleweed." Dan jeers, "I ran all the way home. Hey ya better turn off those cartoons and do yer homework, or yer gonna be stuck in this place, like I told ya'" Dan demands, as he clangs pans together looking for the right one to prepare dinner.

"I'm not ever leaving this place, Mom's here, this is home." his brother defends.

"Jordan, Mom's not here!" Dan exclaims.

"That's not what Shondo said!" the little boy informs.

"Hey, I told you, stay away from that old Medicine Man. He's gonna kill you or worse, he's gonna turn you into a skunk. How'd ya like to go 'round the village stinkin' everything up?" Dan torments.

"He's teaching me the old ways. We gotta know our old ways, I feel it in my heart."

"Feel it in yer heart? You better watch out, the spirit world is dangerous." Dan warns.

"I've been to the ceremonies lots of times and it ain't no fun time. I've seen spirits do things that would make ya go run screaming home."

"Nuh-uh!" Jordan responds, "Our ways are good. They teach to respect one another and to rely on the Creator. I've heard it from more than one."

"I don't know which ceremonies you are talking about, but our ways tell how to stay in harmony without givin' up who we are; and to do whatever it takes to survive!" Dan exclaims.

The door slams.

"What the hell are you two arguing about? I can hear ya hollering halfway down the road!" their father attacks.

Ben no longer appears as the once happy husband, but a tired unpleasant man.

"You aren't done with dinner yet, boy?" Ben asks.

"I've been working on it, I ran all the way home right out of school." Dan defends.

"I told you, I want supper done when I walk in the door." Ben demands.

"What da ya want, raw mutton?" Dan remarks.

The masculine father quickly steps up in front of Dan and slaps him across his cheek.

"Shut yer smart mouth boy."

Dan raises both arms to protect his face.

"I didn't raise no smartass!" he insists.

"I'm sorry, I'm sorry Daddy." Dan replies.

"Get that food cooked and on the table, and give me a beer!" Ben adds. "Stinkin' mine coats ya throat with charcoal!"

Ben grabs the beer out of Dan's hand and swings around facing Jordan.

"Turn those damn cartoons!" he screams at the terrified little boy.

Jordan jumps up, "Yes sir. What do ya wanna watch Daddy?" inquires the little boy.

"Just turn it." Ben demands.

Jordan flips through several channels and then stops.

The television is fixed on a man behind a podium.

"Jesus will give you a new heart and make you clean, if you just ask him." informs the TV preacher.

"Turn that squat, turn it!" Dad sharply demands.

"Maybe ya need a new heart Daddy, that's what Mom always said." innocently Jordan suggests.

Dan's eyes rise in fear of what's next.

"Jordan give me that damn remote, before I tear yer ass up!"

Jordan walks halfway to his father and tosses the remote the other half. The father juggles the remote trying to gain control of it, all the while the preacher preaches.

"You can't run from God. He knows everything about you." the preacher states.

"See, ya can't run from God Daddy, that's what Mom used to always say." Jordan confirms, with a halfway expression of disgust.

"That damn Jesus stuff got yer mother killed! I told her it would!" proclaims Dad, in an emotional voice of dejection.

Jordan's head falls, his spirit completely broken. Jordan just stands there.

Dad demands, "Go help yer brother with supper, I'm starvin'."

Jordan shuffles across the floor to the table where Dan is setting the plates. Dan reaches around Jordan and embraces him from the side,

"Hey big guy, Mom's proud of you. But you know about that Jesus stuff, ya can't listen to it. Mom told me for years, but it just didn't mean anything. You've gotta git a hold of our religious ways to make Daddy happy. Mom and Becky have been gone two years now. They can't help with Daddy anymore. We've just gotta face it, Mom was wrong."

"Shut up, Momma was never wrong about anything! Take it back, take it back you squat hole!" Jordan sternfully pleads.

"Okay, okay, I'm sorry, I take it back." Dan whispers, "Quiet down before Daddy tears up both our rears."

"Was Mom really wrong about that Jesus?" Jordan seriously inquires in a quiet innocent tone.

"No ….I don't know…., I'm sure she wasn't." Dan wonders.

"It really didn't mean anything to you all those years? Her words didn't mean anything?" Jordan asks in bewilderment.

"Wipe yer eyes, don't let Daddy see you like that." Dan comforts, his motion slowing as he contemplates his little brother's question.

Jordan runs the back of his wrist back and forth across his nose and then twists the lower part of his palms against his eyes.

"You alright?" Dan asks. Jordan nods in confirmation.

"Supper's ready." Dan proclaims.

Chapter Four

Instinctive

The small living room in the shabby house is black. Footsteps enter the room. There is the sound of bumping against furniture, then shuffling papers and finally a click.

The room brightens from the glow of the television set. The light shines across Dan standing close in front of the TV in nothing but a pair of blue jean shorts. His skinny brown frame shines to the bright hew of the entertainment box.

"So come in today to Craaazy Jack's!" Dan quickly lowers the blaring volume, "and buy yer next pre-used car from us. We guarantee yer satisfaction or we'll double a quarter of yer money back! How's that for a sure-fire guarantee?" the TV car salesman assures.

The remote clicks.

"Welcome back to Mystery Monster Theatre." the creepy TV voice calls. The TV remote clicks.

"Your soul is the most important thing to God." assures the television evangelist. "Imagine to be tormented forever in the place called hell." warns the black suited TV evangelist, standing behind a shiny wooden pulpit in front of tall maroon velvet curtains.

Dan sits down on the wooden floor just feet from the television set.

"You wouldn't want your worst enemy to endure one minute in that place. Why would you send yourself there for all eternity?" asks the preacher.

"Don't you want to be in the beautiful place called heaven with all your family members instead?

Wouldn't your mother be thrilled to see you enter heaven? There she is at those pearly golden gates, waiting for you. Are you going to disappoint her?" inquires the preacher.

"All ya have to do is believe. You know, trust in something higher than yourself. It's actually pretty easy, all you have to do is say Jesus, I'm a sinner. I've done a lot of things that are wrong, please forgive me, Jesus, I believe you are the Son of the Living God without sin and you died on a cross in my place so I could have eternal life in heaven, please come into my heart and save me.

That's all ya have to say, now believe it down deep and He'll give you a new heart." the preacher instructs.

Dan mutes the TV and looks up. "Ma, I know it meant a lot to you. Ma I'm scared!" he closes his eyes.

"Jesus, my ma believed in you an awful lot. That preacher said you died for us. Well she died for you. She thought so highly of you she gave all her kids Bible names. I don't know if that means much to you, it meant everything to her.

Jesus, I don't know what it's all about, but I know my ma wasn't lying to me all those years." Dan assures.

"I've been taught since I was younger than Jordan that it's wrong to believe in the white God. A

51

bunch of our people paid for it. Momma taught one way and Daddy taught another.

I know all about our Nawhe spiritual ways, but I only know a little about your ways.

Daddy hated for Mom to say anything about the Christian way, but she taught me enough that says you're a good God.

Our ways are confusing. Sometimes the spirits are mean, it's like they're missing something. We've been doing these things for hundreds of years, and we're still here, isn't that good?

We have good times when we come together. We laugh and eat during our celebrations, but our ceremonies are something different. They always give me a feeling of uneasiness, like we're doing something wrong. I know it's not just me, why should our ceremonies be so dark?

I know Mom always said it's about caring for everyone and loving the Creator that made us. We respect the spirits cause they protect us. But I believe what Ma said about you, you love us.

Momma said you died on that cross so we could really know our Creator. She loved you and Creator. I think she would have even loved those that killed her and my sister.

It doesn't make any sense! How can you have that kinda love? I want to know, Jesus I want to know!" He puts his hands together in a tight grip.

"Well here goes" Dan nervously announces, "Jesus, my people are against you, but my mother wasn't." he begins to pray softly, "I believe in you right now. I believe you are God's Son. I believe you did no wrong and I believe you died for my sins." Dan pants. "Will you please come into my heart and save me and be real to me like you were real to Ma, amen." Dan pleads.

After a few second of silence Dan feels warmth in his heart, he looks at his chest as if something is touching him, the warmth turns to pain.

"Ow, ow" Dan lightly cries. "What the…….. He grimaces and clutches his chest. "Ow, I didn't mean kill me!" Dan jokes.

After a few seconds the pain subsides. Dan's face starts to glow and his eyes widen and are filled with joy and wonder.

"What is going on? Man this feels good! Wow it's like what problems? incredible, amazing!" Dan whispers.

"Amazing, this is what Mom meant, He is real! I actually feel different in my heart. I … I understand now."

Dan looks up, it seems the room is spinning as he raises his arms while yet on his knees.

Looking down on Dan from above reveals the bliss on his face as the room spins from his supernatural experience. The room goes dark.

The smell of bacon and coffee drift downs the hall to awaken Ben, as the sun is just creating a morning hew outside.

Ben rises out of his slumber and makes his way down the darkened hallway stopping at the bathroom.

After a few moments the sound of the commode flushing and water running can be heard.

The door opens and he quickly reenters the hall and staggers toward the kitchen.

"You're up awfully early." Dad remarks, "heard ya up late too."

"Sorry Dad, I didn't mean to bother you." Dan apologizes.

"I can't complain much with a bacon and egg breakfast before work. Gimme some of that coffee, son." Dad asks.

Dad pulls out a chair at the small table and sits down to the creaking of his chair.

Dan slides two eggs onto Dad's plate and then fills his father's cup with steaming hot coffee.

Dan asks, "Dad, do you miss Mom and Becky?"

"Of course I do! What kind of stupid question is that?" Dad bristles, the tension in the room immediately rises.

"We don't talk about them much anymore. Isn't that kinda bad?" Dan asks.

"Boy, we don't talk about it cause it upsets Jordan." Dad defends.

"Jordan loves to talk about them. He says he's never leaving this place, because Mom's here." Dan informs with a saddened face.

"Stupid kid, Mom and Becky are buried out there at the cemetery. They've gone on to the spirit world, you know that." Dad reminds, "You have been to our ceremonies plenty of times, since you became a man.

You know that the spirits of the dead are all around us and in the caves and hills. They are here to help us hunt, and pray for us to Conga to heal us when we're sick."

Dan's eyes sparkle and he argues, "But Mom and Becky, both didn't believe our traditional ways, they believed in…"

"Don't say it boy, I told you it was Jesus that got them killed! I told them, time and time again, don't share that squat with the villagers, but she wouldn't listen to me! I begged her, even cried, she still said

55

she had to. It was out of my hands, you know our ways, I told both of them, that's why I never let you and Jordan go.

I told her the girl is hers, but you boys were my responsibility. I took you to the ceremonies as soon as I could, and tomorrow night we'll take Jordan." Dad proclaims.

"No, I mean you know Mom wouldn't like that." Dan rejects.

"Didn't you just hear me boy? It was never up to yer Mom, this is my responsibility!" Dad sternly points out.

"But ...he's too little. I only started going a couple of years ago!" Dan reasons.

"There's no point waiting. We can't keep leaving him home by himself." Dad argues.

"But he'll be scared!" Dan tries to argue.

"It's our spirit world. He's gotta learn sometime." Dad determines, as he shovels in his breakfast.

"I don't want to go!" Dan blurts out, as he puts his fingers to his heart and rubs.

"What!" Dad screams, almost chocking on his bacon,

"You've never missed a ceremony before. You are on your way to being the youngest shaman, since

Shondo. Why don't you want to go?" Dad forcefully inquires.

"I've got a lot of extra homework that Miss Sims has given me." pointing at his school book on the table, "She says if I plan on being a world traveling reporter, I'll have to do a bunch of extra paperwork before school's out this year."

"I told you boy, yer not going off on no plane or no college. You'll be there tomorrow night. Miss Sims can use her extra paperwork to keep herself warm this winter!"

As Dad gets up he knocks his chair backwards to the floor, the chair bangs and rattles on the wooden floor. "I don't want to hear another word about it!" Dad finalizes as he grabs and opens his lunch box.

Dad shoves several pieces of bread and some left over mutton into his box.

"You get your rear home in time to feed Jordan and get to the ceremonial grounds tomorrow night, you hear me?!" Dad demands.

"Yes sir, I hear ya." Dan returns in a decidedly disgusted voice.

Dad looks intently at the young man as he rushes through the screen door slamming it behind him.

"Jesus I can't go, I know it!" Dan cries shaking his head in disagreement.

Chapter Five

Intimidation

The school bell rings. Another day ends as the kids once again bound down the school steps and gleefully race for home.

"Why ya draggin' ya feet Dan, let's go!" Carl questions as they begin to exit the school building into the bright sunny daylight.

"You go ahead. I have to talk to Miss Sims." Dan answers, holding open the door.

"Why don't ya just marry her and get it over with already!" Carl jokes, gesturing with his hand for Dan to go back inside.

"Whatever. I'll see ya tomorrow." Dan calls.

"Hey speaking of tomorrow. Are ya gonna walk out to the ceremony with me and Dad tomorrow?" Carl asks. Carl stops walking backwards waiting for a response from Dan.

Younger children press past Dan and run down the steps.

"I don't know." Dan stutters, poking and rubbing his heart with two fingers.

"Com'on, you can't walk by yourself. You know your ol' man will stop out there on the way from work. He's not coming all the way home to walk all the way back out there, he never does." Carl informs.

"You know your Dad and I don't get along. Every time I run by the bar he and his buddy's are staring at me like they'd like to kill me!" Dan voices.

"Bull squat, Dan. You're just letting your imagination run wild!" Carl states. "And another thing, you know you can't go by Shondo's place by yerself. Dad said the old man lost his mind and is a renegade shaman. You know there's nothing worse than a medicine man gone mad. If he catches you he'll probably turn yer body into a zombie and make your head into a raven!" Carl intimidates.

"Alright, I'll think about it. I'll see ya tomorrow." Dan calls.

"Well kiss her once for me, Miss Sims that is." Carl ridicules.

"Ha, Ha!" Dan sarcastically replies.

Dan steps into the doorway of the school and watches Carl rush off. He steps back out the door and stealthily walks across the broad dirt street to the little white tattered church.

Dan reaches the opposite side of the church from any onlookers and peers in a dirty window. The sanctuary seems dark worn and dated. Dan looks into the mysterious structure that he has regarded with great discontentment for years, especially the last two.

He keeps searching until he sees the pastor. Dan watches as the minister walks into a back room.

As Dan makes his way along the outer wall of the church, a lizard scurries along the foundation of the building running from Dan's pursuit of the side door.

He presses his body against the wall and peers in the dusty glass window.

Dan gradually turns the door knob until the door opens. He then cautiously pushes the door open to a few squeaks of the hinges.

Dan grits his teeth and quickly enters the church, attempting to hide himself from any outsiders. He closes the door rapidly with a gentle quick nudge.

The teenager looks around and sees no one as he begins to make his way slowly across the sanctuary floor.

As he approaches the door opening the pastor entered moments earlier he slows and peeks in.

The room is somewhat dark and as his eyes are trying to adjust to the lack of light, he thinks he sees someone in another room adjoining the office.

He begins to take another step when someone grabs him by the shoulder. He jumps and drops his school books as he swings around abruptly.

Dan finds himself staring at the tall broad shouldered pastor face to face.

"Can I help you son?" the rich voiced man inquires.

"Holy mackerel!" Dan blurts out, "Oh I'm sorry, Pastor! You scared the daylights outta me!"

"I'm sorry, Dan, I should have called to you." the minister apologizes.

"You know my name Pastor?" Dan surprised, asks.

"Of course I know all your family. Your Mom and sister had gone to church here for years. They prayed for you, Jordan and Ben all that time. I'm very sorry for your Mom and Becky. I wasn't allowed to go to the funeral."

"Yeah, I know, I'm sorry about that, Pastor Knows." Dan apologizes, bowing his head.

"It wasn't your fault son. I know some of the tribe's ways, too." Pastor remarks. "Well, tell me Dan, what do I owe to the great honor of a visit from a future shaman to my humble church?"

"Well sir…." Dan hesitates, "I umm…"

"Go ahead, what is it son?" the pastor encourages.

"I think, I'm a…, like I feel um…, I think I'm a Christian!" Dan proclaims.

Pastor Knows coughs, caught off guard, "You're a what?" he asks.

"I'm a Christian!" Dan proclaims again.

"You're a Christian? You weren't a Christian the last I knew." Pastor Knows recalls.

"Well you know Ma talked to me about it since I could remember. We read the Bible and sang those songs and stuff. But when I got older" Dan continued, "Dad caught us singin' and Bible readin' and stuff, he blew up. He told Ma to stop convertin' me. He said I was supposed to be Nawhe, not no Christian. He told Mom, he gave her Becky, but me and Jordan were his." Dan recites.

"I knew all that, Dan, but what happened that you're a Christian now?" Pastor asks.

"Well yesterday, me and Jordan was talking about Ma and Becky. I got to thinking about it, I couldn't sleep, it was eatin' at me, so I got up after everybody went to sleep and watched this preacher on TV. He said some stuff I remember Ma sayin'. He said Mom would be proud of me, and he said if I just believed,... well I believed as hard as I could, and when I prayed to Jesus, somethin' happened."

The Pastor smiled and tears begin to well up in his eyes as he tightens his lips.

"Your Mom is proud of you Dan. She prayed for this day for 15 years before she died, and Becky too."

"I know Pastor, but something weird happened last night when I prayed. When I was done prayin', my heart start burnin, then it started hurtin' like I was havin' a heart attack. Then I felt so good, and now I don't want to do some stuff I used to do before."

"Your heart was hurtin', I mean hurting?" Pastor asks.

"Uh huh, I mean, yes sir." Dan admits.

"That's amazing, do you know what that means Daniel?" Pastor asks.

"Uh no, that's one of the reasons I came over here, was to ask you what it was." Dan inquires.

"Daniel, Daniel, there's a couple of things. One when you ask Jesus to forgive you of your sins, he comes and cleanses your heart. He takes out the old and begins to make room for Himself, and something incredible is…is.." Pastor pauses.

"What Pastor? Is what?" Dan impatiently asks.

"Sit down Daniel." they both take a seat in the front pew of the old musky sanctuary.

"Daniel," the pastor continues to hesitate and think.

"I'm not sure I should tell you." Pastor wonders.

"What, is it bad, sir?" Dan asks.

"Well no, I mean, it's complicated, it's easy for me to tell you, but…" Pastor hesitates.

"It's our ways isn't it?" Dan asks.

"Yeah, it's your ways and your people." Pastor stops and lowers his head.

"Let me tell you something Pastor, the way I feel right now, I gotta know. I know about our people and the Christians. My Dad was saying just this morning that's why Ma and Becky got killed. But still I gotta know, I don't feel the same way I did yesterday. Something is really eatin me up, tell me Pastor what is it?"

"Daniel" Pastor begins, "I want you to take this real slow. I've seen people experience Jesus and just can't stop."

"What do ya mean, can't stop?" Dan wonders, listening intently with great concern for the answer.

"I'm sorry Daniel, I don't mean to frighten you. It's nothing bad, it's just this place." Pastor explains. "You see what you experienced is something very powerful. It's kinda like some of the things that happen at the ceremonies, but this is something very very good. I don't mean to criticize your ways."

"No, no I know what ya mean." Dan interrupts.

"I've seen things for years that just aren't good. I know that now. Last night after what happened I knew it in a second. The things we do and the spirits we know, they are not good, I know that now." Dan shamefully admits.

"I see, yes, you're right with the Nawhe, it's very hard. This is the fifth Native Church that I've pastored. Not all tribes are the same. With a couple of the tribes we were able to use some of the cultural ways to honor Jesus, because in their ways they acknowledge a Creator that is very identical to our Father God. So the transition to His Son is something many tribes can accept. The spiritual ways here are very dark, people are led to honor spirits that aren't from God. I don't want to disrespect your ways, but many pastors have been told what happens at the ceremonial grounds, Daniel, they're very evil." Pastor Knows warns.

"Yes, I have no doubt, it's like my eyes are open now. Before, I just followed because it was our way, but now ... now. It's like running toward a cliff in the dark, but now it's daylight and I'm taking a different path." Daniel relates as the knowledge opens his mind.

"I see, OK, Daniel, let me just tell you like it is." Pastor begins again, "When you experience that burning and hurting in your heart, God was transforming you. Again he took out the evil and replaced it with good, but that was only the beginning. You see when you experienced what you did, usually, not always, but usually, you wind up doing great work for God."

"What do you mean great work?" Dan asks.

"Well Dan, usually God anoints you for a higher calling. Some people don't really notice it as much or dismiss it, because there are other things going on at the time and it's not as noticeable. But the more you feel it the more He's going to do something with you.

Now Daniel let me warn you, like your Dad said, your people actually kill the Christians that try and make a difference. That is what happened to your Mother and Becky." Pastor explains.

"Daniel I would be breaking my oath to God if I told you not to do something, but Dan, I was the one who found your Mom and Becky. It destroyed me, I couldn't preach for two months after that happened. It's not like I've got a big congregation, but still they are my sheep." Pastor Knows continues.

"What happened to you was spiritually you were blind, but now you see. God gave you a new heart, you can't deny the truth. Usually what happens is you grow hungry for the Word, the Bible. They are God's own words, and your spirit has been reborn and it wants God's Word. The more you read the more you'll be changed. God will allow you to remember his words when you need them to live by and testify of Him. And what's going to happen Daniel is you'll want to share God's Word with people. And that's where the problem lies.

Daniel if this happens like I just said, promise me, I mean promise me son, that you'll take it slow. You know how dangerous it is, I owe it to your Mother to protect you and give you good guidance. Please Daniel don't tell anyone you're a Christian. It's going to happen, if you're truly are a Christian, it's going to happen, you can't hold it in. Because Jesus said if you are ashamed of me before men, I'll be ashamed of you before my Father which is in heaven. Just take it slow Daniel, promise me, just take it slow." The pastor tearfully pleads with Dan.

"I promise you Pastor Knows, I'll take it slow. I don't know how I'm special and can do anything for God, but I'll take it slow, I promise." Dan commits.

"Believe me Daniel, God is going to have you do something special. I can genuinely feel it, you are anointed by God. Wait just a moment, let me give you something." the minister jumps up and rushes to his office, he quickly emerges from the dark room once again.

"Here Daniel this belongs to you." He hands Dan a leather bound Bible with a silver cross on the front cover.

"It was your mother's." Pastor tells, "I was the one who found them that night."

Dan pulls the book to his chest.

"I don't know why I picked it up and kept it, it should have gone to the family, but I just couldn't put it back down. She would have wanted you to have it Daniel. "

Tears form in Dan's eyes.

"I remember it. She always kept it on the nightstand besides her bed. When Dad wasn't around she would read to us from its pages. She read the words like they were alive. I think I know what she was saying now." Daniel affirms.

"Pastor, I gotta go, I appreciate your help, but there's one more thing I have to know." Dan thinks.

"Anything." Pastor agrees.

"Well, I told you I don't want to do stuff I used to do. Tomorrow night we have ceremonies and I can't do it. Every time I think about it, something in me just says "no." But Daddy said I have to be there, he's not taking "no" for an answer, what should I do Pastor?" Dan reverently asks.

"Daniel, that's one of the things I was telling you. You're going to have to take it slow. If you don't go, your father is going to know something is up. Can't you just go and maybe God will make a way as time goes along?" Pastor instructs.

"I know you're right Pastor, but I really feel I shouldn't." Dan states in frustration, "I don't think you know what goes on out there. It's not the right spirit, I know that now."

"Daniel what you're going to have to do is ask God to protect you. Be the light in the darkness, OK?" Pastor asks.

"Sure, hey I better get outta here. I'm way late, thanks again Pastor." Dan says.

"God bless you son." Pastor Knows calls.

Dan bursts from the church door and runs down the dusty windy road, his mind is buzzing with all that Pastor Knows has told him and he feels he has a new treasure in his arms, his mother's Bible.

Again he passes the bar, and again there are the same threesome staring him down. But this time Dan looks boldly at each of them and smiles, "beautiful day" Dan calls.

The three men look at one another inquisitively. Dan continues to run. He's hoping his father hasn't got home yet, but he knows better.

Dan approaches his house, he tucks his new Bible in between his other two books. He jumps on the porch and slowly opens the screen door. Before he can completely enter the house his father confronts him.

"Where the hell have you been?!" his father screams and draws his arm around from his side then quickly swings it around like a wrecking ball and slaps Dan in the face knocking him to the floor, his books go skidding across the floor.

"Your brother has been here by himself all this time and there's no supper!" Dad rages. "What have you been doing, boy?"

"I'm alright Daddy." Jordan assures. His father ignores the little boy's comment.

In the mean while, Dan hurries to conceal his mother's Bible, now in clear sight.

"Are you and that Douglas boy hangin' around after school smoking cigarettes again?"

"No Daddy. We were just talkin' was all. I lost track of time, I'm sorry."

Dan quickly scoops up his books from the floor and tucks them away on a small shelf in a smooth fluid move.

"I'll get supper started right now, I won't be long." Dan says, holding his aching head and stinging cheek.

"Boy, I'm not always gonna be here to keep an eye on you two. You better grow up and realize that!" Dad threatens.

Night has fallen, and the room is dark once again. In the dark house, a light goes on. There is a dull glow in the bedroom. Dan is inspecting the words of his new Bible under a blanket with a flashlight. He reads "I am the vine; you are the branches. If a man remains in me and I in him, he will bear much fruit; apart from me you can do nothing.

If anyone does not remain in me, he is like a branch that is thrown away and withers; such branches are picked up, thrown into the fire and burned.

If you remain in me and my words remain in you, ask whatever you wish, and it will be given you. This is to my Father's glory, that you bear much fruit, showing yourselves to be my disciples."

Dan hears a rustling noise in the room. He turns off his flashlight and slowly peeks out from under the blanket. He glances at Jordan rolling over in his bed.

He realizes if he's caught with this Bible it could mean more than the slap on the check he got earlier from his Dad.

When he is sure there is no further possible intruder he goes back to his reading. The flashlight brightens the room again. "As the Father has loved me, so have I loved you. Now remain in my love.

If you obey my commands, you will remain in my love, just as I have obeyed my Father's commands and remain in his love. I have told you this so that my joy may be in you and that your joy may be complete.

My command is this: Love each other as I have loved you. Greater love has no one than this, that he lay down his life for his friends. You are my friends if you do what I command.

I no longer call you servants, because a servant does not know his master's business. Instead, I have called you friends, for everything that I learned from my Father I have made known to you.

You did not choose me, but I chose you and appointed you to go and bear fruit—fruit that will last. Then the Father will give you whatever you ask in my name. This is my command: Love each other."

Dan repeats, "If you remain in me and my words remain in you, ask whatever you wish, and it will be given you. Greater love has no one than this, that he lay down his life for his friends."

You did not choose me, but I chose you and appointed you to go and bear fruit—fruit that will last. Then the Father will give you whatever you ask in my name. This is my command: Love each other."

"Yes Jesus, I will" Dan commits.

He stays up for hours reading and absorbing the words on many pages. "I will give you the keys of the kingdom of heaven; whatever you bind on earth will be bound in heaven, and whatever you loose on earth will be loosed in heaven."

Chapter Six

Revelation

"Daniel, Daniel, did you hear what I asked, or are you daydreaming of an airplane again?" Ms. Sims asks.

"Wha, what Ms. Sims?" Dan asks.

"I thought so Daniel Morgan." the pretty petite sandy haired white teacher affirms. "I asked who is the greatest orator of America?"

"Chief Joseph." Dan answers.

The class bursts into laughter.

"Good answer, but no, the greatest orator of America was…" Ms. Sims stops as the bell rings.

The children all begin to collect their books and run out the classroom door.

"Alright, we'll discuss the answer tomorrow. Think about it, good afternoon children." Ms. Sims calls.

The children again scurry out of the school building and head home.

"Ooo, busted again, Big Dan. What was ya dreaming about this time, flying like an eagle, or dancing like a turkey?" Carl laughs.

"No nuthin' like that." Dan replies.

"Hey Carl do you ever think about God?" Dan questions as he stares at the little white church across the street.

"God?" Carl questions, "Ya mean Conga? Of course. What kinda Nawhe would I be if I didn't think about Conga? As a matter of fact are ya walking out to the ceremonies with me and Dad tonight?"

"Naw, I gotta stop by the house and get Jordan." Dan says.

"Jordan, yer takin' Jordan? He's too little. Why are ya takin him? He's gonna get his pants scared off 'em, you know that!" Carl claims.

"Yeah I know, but Dad doesn't want him to stay home by himself. Ol' Lady Talltree doesn't like us getting in late and pickin' him up. Besides Dad wants him to start early for some reason." Dan declares.

"Ya mean you guys are gonna walk by Shondo's place by yerself? Do you know what that medicine man is gonna do to you guys if he catches ya? He'll take off body parts and hang them around the outside of his porch to set an example of ya. He'll probably make ya the walkin' dead. Then you'll come to my window and try'n get me. But I'm gonna blow yer head off with a shotgun, best friend or no best friend. My luck you'll probably pick it up and put back on and crawl through the window and…" Carl rattles.

"Are you done? Dude, you need to cut back on the mutton. I told ya about mutton overload. Any way, you know what, a couple of days ago I might have been afraid. But now I'm looking forward to it!" Dan proclaims.

"Are you crazy, looking forward to it? I'm walkin' with my Dad and I'm still scared. Why are ya so brave now big man?" Carl asks.

"That's what I was asking ya earlier, about God. I believe God is real and protects us when we really believe in Him." Dan imparts.

"What, do ya mean Conga? To be honest those spirits scare me. The last time we came home from the ceremonies, I had nightmares every day for a week!" Carl confesses.

"That's what I'm trying to tell ya. I'm not talking about Conga and the spirits. I'm talking about the Christian God, Jesus!" Dan proclaims.

"Jesus!, are you crazy man? Jesus! Why are ya talkin' about Jesus? You've gone to the ceremonies longer than I have. Our ways says that the white man's God is evil. He's against our ways. You know better than most. They say you know more about the spirit ways than a lotta the men. What the crap are you talkin' about Jesus for?" Carl questions.

"Carl, can you keep a secret?" Dan asks, hearing the Pastor's words in his head "take it slow."

Carl says, "Sure, yer my best friend. We have lots of secrets. Like that time we busted out Ol' Lady Talltree's window with a baseball. And that time we stole shotgun shells from the Trading Post, or the time..."

"OK, OK, Carl. But I mean a real secret, it could mean my life if ya told anyone." Dan tells.

"Wow, sounds pretty serious, I promise Dan. I'll keep yer secret. What is it, did ya catch Ms. Sims making out with the janitor?' Carl jokes.

"No, no nothin' like that." Dan looks around like he's selling drugs to a minor. "Ya see I'm a…, I'm a …, well ya see I'm a…" Dan stutters.

"You're a what? You're not funny are ya? I'm tellin' ya Dan, if you're tellin' me yer funny, we can't be friends anymore. Stay in the closet man, just stay in the closet!" Carl frets.

"Don't be stupid! I told ya I like Teresa. Don't gross me out Dude!" Dan defends.

Carl remarks, "Whew, that was close. I was afraid I was gonna have ta, kick yer a…."

"Alright, alright, I told ya I wasn't. Besides I would hope that I could do bettr' 'en you if I was!" Dan comes back.

"Well what are ya then? If yer not funny and it's all that serious." Carl quips, "Are ya not really Nawhe? Are ya moving away, what?"

"OK, I am in the closet, but it's not cause I'm funny it's because, I'm a …Christian." Dan blurts out.

"A Christian? You're a what? No way, what the hell? I think it would have been better if ya said you were funny!" Carl declares, "how, why do ya think yer a Christian?"

"Well, I was talking about Mom with Jordan and Dad and got to thinkin'. Then I watched this TV preacher..." Dan tries to tell.

Carl interrupts, "See! That's why Dad doesn't let us have a TV, right there! Don't get any cartoons, no Gilligan's Island, like my parents got to watch. No MTV, just cause of those preachers. They try to convert ya and the next thing ya know yer dead! This is pretty serious Dan."

"I know, I couldn't stand it. I read Mom's Bible last night for at least five hours. It's all stuck in my head. I can hear the words over and over. I had to tell someone and yer my best friend, please don't tell anyone Carl, OK?" Dan pleads.

"Oh I'm not tellin' anyone that's for sure! I don't want to see ya dead. I wouldn't wish that on anyone!" Carl replies.

"And especially don't tell yer Dad." Dan requests.

"I wouldn't tell Dad for all the shotgun shells in Mississippi!" Carl states. "Hey speakin' of Dad, I've gotta get home, if I'm gonna walk to the ceremonies with him. I ain't walkin' by Shondo's place by myself, that's fer sure!

I'll talk to ya later about this Jesus stuff, but don't go tryin' to convert me. Cause I ain't listenin'. Yer not a Christian, your mind is just playin' tricks on ya.

Anyway, why don't ya stop and tell Shondo yer a Christian? Just kiddin', see ya out there!" Carl yells as he runs down the dirt road.

Dan runs too, he looks for the familiar men at the bar. But this time the men aren't standing outside the bar. He heads home as quickly as he can.

Chapter Seven

Black Journey

The road is dark and there is the sound of every insect and animal along the road as Dan and Jordan walk to the ceremonies.

They are each carrying a large sack on their backs as they approach Shondo's place.

"Dan, why do we gotta carry all this stuff? Its heavy!" Jordan asks.

"It's our garments. Anybody that enters the sacred grounds has to have sacred garments. The longer you go to the ceremonies, the more you'll learn about the secret and importance of the garments. You can start out with my old garments. They're mostly rabbit, squirrel, gopher and quail feathers. Some of the men will wear animals and feathers that are more significant to the tribe, you'll see.

Now Jordan some of the men are gonna be really scary and stuff is gonna happen. Stuff you've never seen before, just don't be scared. I'll stay right by ya and Daddy will be there too. But even he's gonna do stuff that might scare ya.

Just stay to the outside of the circle and don't let anyone get too close to ya. If ya have to, run Jordan!" Dan warns.

"I'm already I' scared!" Jordan admits. "Why couldn't I just stay home?"

"I don't know Jordan. That probably would have been best, but you know Daddy" Dan says. "Wait, be quiet, there's Shondo's house. Walk real quiet Jordan. If he finds us out here by ourselves, that's it, we're done for!"

"I thought you said you weren't scared. Why are you so afraid of Shondo? He's always good to me. We talk all the time." Jordan conveys.

"Yer dreamin'! When have you ever talked to Shondo?" Dan asks.

"I've talked to him lots of times. Ever since Momma and Becky went away. I 'member the first time. It was a couple of days after they went to the spirit world. I was missin' them really bad. I was cryin' really bad all day and even at night. You went to sleep. I kept askin' Momma and Becky to come back. Daddy told me earlier that day they weren't ever comin' back and I had to get over it. But I just kept cryin'. It was really late and I wasn't cryin' as hard." Scenes of that night begin to flash back in Jordan's mind.

"The house was really quiet. I was 'memberin' when Momma would come down the hall when I would cry. She would always come in the room and come and sit on my bed with me and hum some pretty song. I was cryin' and just askin' and askin' if she would come and sing to me just one more time. I laid there hopin' really hard that she would. Then I heard footsteps comin' down the hall." As he speaks, Jordan sees the images of his dark bedroom dimly lit by the outside moon. He remembers looking over his blanket curled in his hands toward the olive green door at the approaching footsteps.

"At first I thought it was Daddy, but I could tell it wasn't. I knew Momma's footsteps, they came right to the door. I could hear the door knob turnin'. I knew it was Momma, so I said real quiet "Momma" and the door began to open real slow."

The little boy's eyebrows raised in anticipation, he didn't know whether to be excited, afraid or just scream. "I looked over at you, but you were snoring like a train. Then there was a figure standing there, but it wasn't Momma, it was Shondo!"

"What!" Dan screams, forgetting where he was, "Oh squat, get down!" as Dan throws he and Jordan into the small brush.

"Quiet......" Dan whispers harshly looking towards Shondo's house, to see if they have been discovered.

"What? You're lying. Shondo's never been in our house!" Dan says in bewilderment.

"But, he was." Jordan confirms, "He was right there standing in our bedroom door. I was so scared when I saw him. He was dressed like an old 'ndan. He had long grey hair. I didn't know who he was. All I knew was there was a strange man in our bedroom and I was expectin' Momma. I was so scared I couldn't say anything. I couldn't scream. I couldn't move anything but my eyes. I looked over at you and you were still snoring. I was so mad at you for being asleep. I was screaming at ya with my eyes. I was scared. I opened my mouth finally to scream and nothing came out. He walked in the door right towards me. I was gonna throw the covers over my head, but I knew I would die anyway, so I wanted to see him kill me."

Jordan's mind recalls the images that night, the old man dressed in full buckskin with long fringes walks as a stealth cat and reaches Jordan's bed side.

"But then" Jordan pauses, "he smiled with a nice smile and kneeled by my bed and said in Nawhe.

"Jordan, it's alright. Your Momma and Becky sent me to you. They said they couldn't come, but they want you to know they miss you too and they're alright."

Then the old man's voice changes to that of Jordan's Momma and says, "Don't cry, my baby. It's OK. You take care of Daniel and Daddy. It won't be long and me and Becky will see you soon." Shondo said for Mom.

"I wasn't scared at all after that."

He blessed me with his hands on my head and cheek. He got up and walked over to you, you were still sawing logs.

I sat up and watched him, he put his hands on your head and cheek and prayed something. He turned around and smiled again and said, "Rest now"

"Before I saw him go out the door I was asleep." Jordan finishes.

"You were asleep alright. You dreamed the whole thing!" Dan ridicules.

"Nuh-uh, it did happen. Let's just go ask Shondo, he'll tell ya." Jordan challenges.

"Shut up, that old medicine man will call you a liar and eat both of us!" Dan growls. "Now, come on, let's get outta here before he hears us."

As he finished the sentence, they heard a wolf barking and growling from the little house of the Shaman.

"Oh sq…uat, run Jordan! Run! He's turned into a wolf!" Dan shouts.

They run frantically down the road. Dan is practically carrying Jordan by the scuff of the neck as they run. Adrenaline pumps through their bodies to the point their feet are scarcely touching the ground. They run farther and farther into the darkness.

The night is practically pitch dark, the sound of footsteps stop on a black trail.

"Put your sack down right here." Dan orders.

Dan lights a match and places it to a kerosene lantern.

"Ya mean we had a lantern all this time and ya didn't light it?" Jordan asks. "We tripped over every rock and bush in the trail and you had a lantern?"

"Ya can't, not until ya get here." Dan says, "They call it the "Black Journey." Ya have ta come at night in the dark. It's a spiritual thing. We all walk the black journey. Our eyes are closed to the spiritual things. It's only when we reach the spirit world can you see. A little ways down this path and you'll see alright.

Now we have to put on our Sacred Garments, here I'll help ya" Dan pulls out all the garments and separates them. He tells Jordan to strip down to his underwear. Dan begins the ritual of making ready.

This is the systematic process of applying the sacred garments while praying to the spirits. Daniel paints Jordan with white chalk from head to toe, then he ties the furs to him. He paints red and black marks across his stomach, chest, arms and face.

91

He chants in Nawhe and makes grunting sounds as he fastens a small bustle of quail feathers to his head.

Dan stops his chanting and begins to pray and ask Jesus to forgive him, "Jesus please, this is wrong, protect me and Jordan and Dad."

"This isn't right, I can sense the spirits down the path. They want blood, help us Jesus!" he prays secretly.

Then he begins to dress himself. When he is done he is covered with a coyote skin and painted black from head to toe, with a few white and red paint stripes across his face, arms and stomach.

He takes a small shield and a short knife and hands them to Jordan, "Here." Dan says.

Then he draws a long knife made of bone out of his bag, and a tall shield, with animals painted upon it.

"Ok, Jordan let's go. Don't be scared. Remember what I told ya. Don't let anyone get too close to ya." Dan demands.

They walk down a path that leads them through tall boulders. There are places that the boulders are narrow and other places where they are wide apart.

Soon Jordan begins to see the drawings on the boulders. Animals and men and some part animal and part man, many drawings of spirits flying and other drawings of battles and dead men.

As they draw closer to the ceremony grounds their lantern is overshadowed by a huge bon fire with many shadows being cast as tall as the boulders and up against the cliff wall. The smell of smoke drifts down the corridor of the path.

As they draw near Jordan takes it all in. He can hear the drumming coming from the center of the ceremonial grounds.

He sees a huge bon fire taller than any of the men, its flames are as a wildfire. Jordan's eyes grow concerned as he sees strange figures about the flames.

As they draw closer he begins to make out the men and older boys dressed as many animals. As he looks toward the arena it looks as if the men become live animals. There he sees a coyote walking on all fours and then standing upright like a man as it begins to dance in honor of the spirits.

On the far side of the group, he sees a black goat and then it too becomes a dancer. He sees several more coyotes and then a huge bear as it tries to attack the other animals and dancers.

Then all a sudden from behind a boulder a Black Panther runs and pounces on the Bear and swipes his claws at his head and shoulder and growls like a great lion. Jordan is in shock, his eyes and mouth wide open.

Dan opens the lantern glass and blows the flame out, he sets the lantern against the wall and tells Jordan, "Stay close to me, just do like I do and remember stay away from everyone else."

So they approach the huge bon fire. Dan begins to dance around and make animal like movements. He points his long knife toward the air around him and strikes his knife back and forth as if to thrust through an enemy.

He backs away as some of the dancers begin to take up his challenge. The two brothers move to the outside of the circle,

"Jordan don't get too close to anyone and don't point your knife directly at them. And whatever ya do don't point, it's a way of criticizing and challenging an enemy. Look there's Dad over there." Dan says, pointing with his lips. "See just point like this." again gesturing with his lips.

Jordan looks to the other side of the arena and sees his Father dress like an elk, with great antlers on his head and a beautiful elk hide all around him.

Jordan is in awe of what he sees . As they dance around the arena Jordan is careful not to let anyone

94

close to him. He feels his eyes are playing tricks on him as the men transform back and forth from animal to human state.

His Dad dances up next to him, "Yer doin' fine son!" Dad calls.

Dan and Jordan try to keep up with their father, but he's too quick, he dashes off like a true elk.

After a while the drummers hit the drum very loudly in quick successive blows and then the arena is quiet. All the dancers spring back from the fire and line the outer edge of the arena.

Three men dressed as deer enter the arena from behind the boulders. They are thin and their legs look like the legs and hoofs of deer from under the deer hides and aprons they wear. They walk like deer to the center of the ceremonial ground.

They each are carrying bowls in both hands. As they reach the center of the arena facing the tall flames, they lift the bowls as in offering.

They make sounds of dying animals and chant in Nawhe. "The life is in the blood, The life is in the blood, The life is in the blood."

The deer dancers then turn around and the drumming starts again in a slow rhythmic pace. The dancers slowly approach the deer in a giant circle around the arena. One by one the men and animals stop at the deer and take a drink of the contents of the bowls.

As they near the deer, Jordan asks, "What is in those bowls?"

Dan replies, "It's deer blood and Indian medicine."

As he says that he hears a voice say, "Do not drink!"

Then Dan hears the voice of Jesus say, "Any man living among you who hunts any animal or bird that may be eaten, must drain out the blood and cover it with earth, because the life of every creature is its blood. That is why I have said, "You must not eat the blood of any creature, because the life of every creature is its blood; anyone who eats it must be cut off." Then the voice goes silent.

Dan turns to Jordan and says, "Don't drink it. They will try to make you. Just put it up to your lips and pretend to drink. Here, Jordan, get in front of me."

As they exchange places, Jordan looks up at his brother as if he is being sacrificed. The line moves quickly as each man takes his drink. Jordan finds himself standing before the Deer Priest. The priest pushes the bowl at Jordan and twists his head side to side with a wild daze in his eyes and angry smirk across his mouth and nose.

Jordan looks into the thick, decorated bowl at the contents of dark rich blood with herbs floating in it. The little boy looks up at the priest and the priest frowns at him. Jordan draws the bowl to his lips and pretends to take a drink. He pulls the bowl away, revealing a ring of blood offering on his lips.

He behaves as if the brew has gagged him. He hands the bowl back to the priest, and the priest smiles with great accomplishment.

Dan steps up to the priest with a stern look upon his face. He quickly takes the bowl from the priest and presses it to his face as if he was taking a big drink, pouring the potion over both edges of the bowl at his mouth. He jerks the bowl back down and forces it to the priest's hands while wiping his mouth with the other hand.

The bowl fumbles in the priest's hands and then falls to the ground. The priest growls at Dan, then Dan quickly kicks dirt over the blood, and walks away.

The priest gestures with his hand and curses at Dan in Nawhe. Dan pushes Jordan away from the crowd.

As all the dancers are served the drumming becomes harder and quicker. The men and animals begin to move quickly around the arena.

Before too long the blood concoction begins to have a hallucinogenic effect on the partakers.

The heads of the dancers begin to swim. They begin to growl and howl as every sort of animal. They begin to run around the arena as a wild herd.

Some leap into the air and run along the boulders and cliff walls, using the walls and boulders as spring boards, swinging their instruments of war.

Jordan and Dan watch in amazement as participants become more engulfed in their ceremony. Before too long Jordan sees a sight he has never experienced before.

Spirits begin coming from every direction. He sees the flying spirits dash in and out of the dancers. The spirits fly around the arena. Some in a quick dashing motion as quickly as the eye can move, others bounce from dancer to dancer and leap through the monstrous fire.

Jordan is astonished at what he sees.

"Danny, Danny I'm scared" cries the little boy.

"It's alright. Let's get outta the way." Dan instructs.

As they attempt to reach the outer edge of the arena, a coyote runs near and strikes Dan with a knife on the arm.   Blood begins to run down his forearm and he knocks Jordan to the ground.

Jordan rolls and jumps back up, "Come on Dan, run!" he screams.

Dan grabs his bleeding arm and staggers off to the arena's edge.   "I'm alright!" Dan tries to put Jordan at ease.

Jordan looks at the blood running down his brother's arm.   His heart is racing and he's panting from all that he has witnessed.   He watches as the dancers work into a frenzy.

He stares at those dancers who leap high into the air. Then something catches his eye in the chaotic scene.

"Look, look!" he calls to Dan, throwing his lips and chin toward the top of a cliff.

Dan looks up from his wounded arm and sees a man dressed as a giant eagle.   Jordan and Dan stare up at the incredible sight.

The man's garments are all eagle feathers from head to toe.   The bright white and black regalia shine by the light of the great fire as the light of day.

Every detail of the man's garments are seen.   His legs are covered with dark feathers and his waist begins to reveal the beautiful white and black eagle feathers. His arms are great wings stretched to his side. His head is like that of a huge eagle, and his eyes roam the ceremonial grounds over his beak as looking for prey.

"Who, who is that?" Jordan asks fearfully.

"That is Shondo." Dan replies.

As they both stare up at him, he spreads his wings and flaps them as he soars to a boulder over 60 feet away. He lands gracefully as a true eagle, flapping more quickly for a soft landing.

The eagle drives all the other animals into a rage.

"Oh my God!" Jordan cries, "I'm outta here!" shaking his head. "I don't care if that is my friend Shondo, let's go!"

"Wait a minute. We can't cross the arena to the entrance now, it's too dangerous. The blood has them going crazy!" Dan warns.

"I don't care. Look at Daddy!" Jordan screams.

They turn to look at their father and he rams the Black Panther dancer, knocking him to the ground.

"Oh no!" Dan yells.

The Panther is dazed by the blow. The Mountain Lion and Bear come to his aid. The threesome come together in conference, and watch the Elk run around the arena.

"Oh no!" cries Dan, "We gotta help Dad. You stay here Jordan, I mean it"!

"No way, if we're gonna die, let's die together!" Jordan yells back.

"I mean it Jordan!" Dan yells as he runs across the arena.

On his way to aid his Father several of the dancers take swipes at Dan with their lances and long knives.

Before he can reach him the three predators tackle the Elk simultaneously. They violently knock him to the ground. They take their clubs and begin to beat him mercilessly.

Dan screams "No… !" as he draws closer to his wounded Dad.

The Panther sees the boy running toward the hunt. The boy is no match for the brutish man. The man draws his club back and steps to the side and clubs Dan with a hard blow as he flies by. Dan lands on the Bear and knocks him to the ground.

They are all piled in a huge ball of fur, flesh and blood. Dan and his father are badly dazed, the Bear, Lion and Panther all rise to their feet and begin to beat on them, to the pleasure of all the other animals.

The animals prance about in laughter and torment. Dan and his father cover themselves, trying desperately to shield themselves from the blows.

Then a little fur figure comes flying in on top of Dan and his Dad, its Jordan. The men stop their beating only for a moment; then the Panther kicks Jordan in the stomach.

"Stop it!', Dan screams "Stop it!."

The trio continues their attack. Dan tries to look for an escape route. He looks up to see Shondo perched on a boulder above them, with his hand reached out to them.

Then it pops into Dan's mind, "I will give you the keys of the kingdom of heaven; whatever you bind on earth will be bound in heaven, and whatever you loose on earth will be loosed in heaven. If two of you on earth agree about anything you ask for, it will be done for you by my Father in heaven."

"Jesus, please get us out of this place, bind these evil spirits and save us!" Dan frantically prays.

Immediately there is a sound of a great wind coming from the boulder trail. The wind begins to howl at it gets closer to the arena.

The wind rises into the air carrying a great cloud of dust and it all lands on the huge bon fire and it goes pitch black.

Chapter Eight

Discovery

The sight of bright light comes through wood slats, while the rhythmic sound of creaking fills the air. The sound of a mosquito buzzes about, slap.

"Damn blood suckers!" Lenny gripes, as the three figures find themselves in their usual afternoon spot on the porch of the bar. Jim is rocking back and forth on an old chair, while Poncho is leaning against the wall like an old cowboy. But in this case a middle aged Indian, and Lenny is sitting with his head on a table made out of an old wooden cable spool.

"I tell ya, somebody was doing some bad medicine last night for that huge bon fire just to go out like that." Poncho notes.

Jim says, "I told ya guys, my boy said that Dan was boasting about bein' a Christian. Maybe Conga was angry that the boy was making a mockery of the ceremonies."

"Yeah" Poncho said, "One of the priests told me that he threw the sacrificial cup on the ground and kicked dirt on it, that's disrespectful. Conga had to be mad about that."

"Just like his mother." Lenny says, "A trouble maker, tryin' to corrupt all the people and ways with that Jesus squat."

Poncho growls, "I better not find out he's a Christian spreading that squat, or he's gonna wind up like his Momma did!"

"Yeah we should just burn their house down with all of 'em in it and be done with it!" Jim says.

"Keep an eye on him. If ya see him doing anything like preachin' to anybody, then we'll take care of it." Poncho says.

"I think that's why Ben attacked you last night. He knows we killed his old lady." Jim tells.

"Of course he knows, ya idiot. He knows what happens to those Christians who try to convert a Nawhe. I told him to shut his old lady up three days before we did her."

"Well maybe after the beatin' the three of them got last night, there's not gonna be anymore Jesus crap." Jim laughs.

"Naw, that family is too hard headed." Poncho warns, "If Conga was that angry about their presence at the ceremonies, something has to be done."

"Well ya know those Christians don't go anywhere without that book. See if the boy has that book." Lenny states.

"Yeah, good idea Lenny. Hey look, here he comes now and there's my boy with him." Jim says in disgust.

Dan and Carl have been talking about what happened last night, too. Dan has been telling Carl about Jesus. As they approach the area in front of the bar their eyes all meet. Instantly, Carl drops his head in guilt.

"Hey boy, get yer rear home, yer ma needs help with dinner!" Jim yells at Carl.

"OK Pa." Carl yells back.

"I told ya be careful around them, they're just lookin' for trouble." Carl states uneasily.

Carl doesn't tell that he let slip to his father that Dan was a Christian while walking out to the ceremonies the night before.

"Come here boy." Poncho calls to Dan.

Dan changes his course and walks directly toward the trio.

"How's ya dad feeling today?" Poncho asks.

"Well he's alright." Dan stammers.

"You tell him for me, that I'm not sore at him for knocking me down last night. I know it was just the excitement going on." Poncho tempts.

"Knock you down?! Yer the ones that attacked us last night!" Dan defends.

"Now ya know boy it's just a part of the ceremony." Poncho further irritates Dan, "It prepares us to always be ready for battle."

"Yeah, well Jesus put a stop to that didn't He?" Dan remarks, without thinking.

"What, what did you say boy? Jesus?" Poncho attacks. "Jesus didn't have anything to do with last night!"

"What do you know about Jesus?" Lenny growls.

"Yeah, what are they teachin' ya in that school of yours?" Jim asks.

"Yeah what are ya readin' there boy?" Poncho asks, gesturing to Dan's books.

"Just English and Algebra." Dan says.

"Well what's this about Jesus yer talking about?" Poncho asks, as he begins to grit his teeth, walking toward Dan.

Dan hears the words of Pastor Knows once again, "take it slow" but these men want to hear about Jesus and Dan is going to tell them.

"Jesus is the true God!" Dan starts, "He gave his life to save us from our sins, He suffered for all of us so we could have a new life." Dan preaches.

"Shut yer mouth boy! Jesus ain't the Nawhe way! That squat is white man's God. We ain't white, we're Nawhe!

You got one chance boy. Walk away and don't say another word!" Poncho demands, "Go home and tell yer Dad what yer preachin' or does he already know?"

Dan smartly steps back, turns around and walks toward home, feeling the eyes of the three men on the back of his head all the way home.

"What have I done?" Dan says to himself, "Pastor Knows told me to take it slow, but the more of the Bible I read the more I can't keep it in. This isn't good. Dad is gonna kill me himself if he finds out, especially tellin' those goons."

Dan reaches his house, steps onto the porch which seems to have grown twice as long and he feels like he is a small child again.

He enters the house and his father greets him, "Hey Dan, ya feeling alright today?

"Oh sure, how are you feeling Dad? You're the one that got the worst of the beatin'." Dan asks.

"I'm doing pretty good. Thanks for wrapping my ribs up last night when we got home. Grab me some ice in a rag and a couple of aspirin, would ya? My head is still killin' me."

"Sure Dad." Dan hurries and gets the items feeling the stress of preaching to their attackers.

"Yeah, you were right Dan. I shouldn't have made Jordan go to the ceremonies last night. He's still too small. He's still sleeping from the beatin'. One of those renegades hit him in the head with his club. I'm gonna find those three and kick the you know what outta 'em!"

"Oh Daddy no!" Dan pleads, "They stopped me in front of the bar and Mr. Darkcloud said he wasn't sore at ya for knocking him down."

"That sorry S-O-B. I'm gonna show him knock down. I'm gonna WWF the squat hole. He thinks he owns the ceremonial grounds just because his garments are the black panther. What he doesn't realize is that the old Nawhe say that symbolizes death, and not just to those he comes in contact with. He is gonna get the worst punishment than anyone." Dad prophesies.

Dan can't hold it in any longer, he feels like he's lying to his Father, he begins to show signs of the strain almost to cry.

"Dad" Dan states hesitantly, "I have to tell you something."

"Yeah what?" Dad grimaces in pain.

"Mr. Darkcloud, Mr. Douglas and Mr. Pipestem was asking me a bunch of questions." Dan says.

"A bunch of questions, what kinda questions?" Dad asks.

"They were asking me what I knew about Jesus." Dan begins.

"Asking ya about Jesus? Why were they asking ya about Jesus? What are those three trying to pull, did ya tell 'em, "not a damn thing?" Dad inquires.

"Well Mr. Darkcloud kept harassing me about last night. He said that beatin' us was just part of the ceremony, and I told him that Jesus put a stop to it." Dan tells.

"What? You told them that Jesus stopped the beatin'? Why would ya say something stupid like that? Jesus didn't have anything to do with that!" Dad violently remarks.

"Yes he did Dad. When we were lying on the ground getting' beat to death, I was really scared. I was afraid they were gonna kill you and me, and Jordan wouldn't have anyone to take care of him. Then when Jordan jumped on top of us and they started beatin' him. I wasn't gonna take it. I couldn't get up, I felt helpless, and they were killin' you. Something popped into my head, Jesus said, "whatever you bind on earth will be bound in heaven, and whatever you loose on earth will be loosed in heaven." Dan relates the scripture from memory.

"Well what makes ya think it was Jesus?" Dad asks.

"Well, because I prayed, Jesus, please get us out of this place, bind these evil spirits and save us, and he did." Dan continues, "Right after I prayed that big wind came and hit the bon fire, and it was pitch black. Those guys quit hittin' us. Then I could feel someone lift me, you and Jordan and it wasn't those three devils. I was so weak, I could barely get up by myself. You thought it was me helpin' ya up and carryin' ya home, but somebody was walking with us.

You were passed out and he carried ya all the way home. I didn't wrap yer ribs. I collapsed as soon as I got in the door. I woke up in my bed this morning and Jordan was in his. You were still passed out when I left for school this morning." Dan explains.

"Well who carried me home and patched my ribs?" Dad asks. "It was probably Jim. He was beatin' us, but he has a big heart too. He's the only one big enough to carry me that far."

"Nope, it wasn't Jim. I could hear him and those other two hollerin', still looking for us, when that guy brought us outta there." Dan said.

"Well who was it then?" Dad asks.

"I don't know, but he was bigger than any guy I've seen in my life. I don't think it was Jesus, it had to be an angel." Dan says.

"An angel? An angel?" Dad pauses, "How did ya ever come to know anything about Jesus in the first place?" Dad inquires.

"Because of Mom." Dan admits, "She used to always read me the Bible and tell me about Jesus. I never believed anything about it, until the other night."

"And just what happened the other night?" Dad demands.

"Well, I was wondering about what Mom used to tell me, and I was watching this preacher on TV." Dan tells.

"Uhuh..." Dad quips shaking his head.

"Well," Dan continues, "He said if ya will really believe in Jesus with all yer heart down deep, then Jesus will give you a new heart and save ya. I know that he did. I've been readin' Mom's old Bible every free minute and everything in it just makes so much sense."

"Where did ya get yer Ma's Bible? I haven't seen it since that night." Dad asks.

"Pastor Knows had it, he said he found them first and picked it up. I seen him the other day, when I had some questions after I became a Christian." Dan says, "He gave it to me."

Dad puts his head down and massages his forehead with his fingers. Dan waits for the explosion. Dad looks to one side then the other with an air of disgust on his face.

"Danny, I've tried everything to keep ya away from that Jesus stuff yer mother tried to push off on me. I took ya to the ceremonies and taught ya all I could about the Nawhe ways. This is your choice, I can't stop ya anymore, yer a man, ya make yer own decisions. Yer Mom did it from the grave. I can't argue after what happened last night. When we were coming home last night I woke up for a couple of seconds, I looked right in the face of that guy carryin' me. I thought I was dreamin'. It was a big white guy like ya said. All I could think was no white man has ever seen our ceremonies. He was smiling at me, it seemed like his face was glowing. I could tell by his eyes he was helping me. My head hurt so bad, I couldn't argue with it and passed out." Dad remembered.

Dan stands in shock of what his Dad just said, not as much about the angel, but more about Dan's acceptance of Jesus.

"We have always said that the white man's God is weak. He might have let them win the big battles and took away our land, but those Christians don't really know about the spirit world. They go to their big beautiful churches and don't even see the spirits that are all around 'em.

Danny, you know how dangerous it is to be a Christian among our people. All I ask is you just don't say anything. Whatever has been said let it lie, take some time to re-cooperate, alright?" Dad asks.

"Alright Daddy, I'll go slow." Dan responds.

"Well, go fix some supper and wake up yer brother." Dad instructs.

"Alright Dad, how's mutton sound?" Dan laughs.

As Dan enters the bedroom, he sees Jordan still in bed.

"Wake up sleepy head, ya can't sleep yer life away." Dan jokes.

"Jordy, Jordan get up" Dan bends over Jordan and shakes him with no response.

"Oh God no!" Dan quivers.

Dan dashes into the living room.

"Dad come quick, there's something wrong with Jordan!"

Ben jumps up and runs to Jordan's side,

"Son wake up!" Dad cries as he shakes the boy. "Come on boy wake up."

Dad places his hand behind Jordan's head to reveal a smudge of fresh blood on his hand, as Dan looks on in horror. Dad puts his ear to Jordan's heart and then his nose.

"Daniel run down to the Tradin' Post and tell old man Reeves that we need his truck to run Jordan to the hospital over in Grants, hurry!" Dad instructs.

Dan burst out the door, practically knocking the screen door off its hinges.

"Please no God, this is my fault, Please no God!" Dan pleads as he kicks up dust running down the dirt road.

Soon old man Reeves and Dan are speeding down the road back toward the little house. The old truck screeches to a halt in front of the house with a great cloud of dust.

Dan jumps out of the truck and runs to the house; and through the dust cloud he sees a small figure standing in the doorway.

"Daddy's gonna be mad at you for breakin' the screen door Daniel." chimes Jordan's little voice.

Dan swoops down and grabs Jordan, holding him tight to his chest.

"Oh you scared me so bad little guy!" Dan cries, with his eyes filled with tears.

"Aw I'm alright. I got to go see Momma and Becky for a little while." Jordan informs.

"Jordan, you went and seen Mom and Becky?" Dan asks.

"Yeah, I was hurtin' really bad and then I got real tired and sleepy. I wanted to stay here, but I could hear Momma calling me, she sounded so sweet." Jordan tells. "So I sat up, but I wasn't in our room. I was sittin' on a real pretty green hill. There were real pretty flowers everywhere. They smelled so good Dan." Jordan says, "I stood up and I could see a little narrow stream just a little ways from me. There were fish in it as big as I am, hundreds of 'em. Danny, I could hear Mom's voice again callin' me.

"Jordy" she said, "there you are." And I looked up and there she was. She was walking toward me real slow with her arms out to me, just smiling her pretty smile. I hollered real loud, "Momma" and I went running toward her. I was running and smiling and crying all at the same time." Jordan tells. "I got to her and jumped into her arms. She swung me around in circles like a merry-go-round. I was so happy we were laughin' and cryin' and talking about how much we missed each other, then Becky was there. She said, "how ya doin' little squirt? "I screamed "Beck...y" she was so beautiful, she was a grown woman. I said, "Becky I've missed you so much, how you used to make cookies for me and tell me funny stories. We talked and talked, and they took me over the top of this hill and Momma said "look Jordan."

But then I heard Daddy calling me, I asked Mommy, "I didn't know Daddy was here?" Momma said, "Baby, you can't stay here, you've got to go back home" I said, but Momma I don't wanna go, I wanna stay with you. She put me down and I could hear Daddy cryin', I hadn't heard Daddy cry in a long time." Jordan says.

"Jordan" Momma comforts, "you've got to be strong now, Daddy and Daniel need you to take care of them, me and Rebecca will be alright, we'll be waiting for you right here."

"I could hear Daddy cryin' "son don't leave Daddy, please don't leave Daddy." He sounded pitiful. Momma and Becky gave me one more hug I began to walk back over where I started from. I looked back and Momma and Becky were holdin' each other by the side. Becky waved at me and Momma blew me a kiss, she said, "see you soon sweetie."

I went and laid down in the same spot where I was. I closed my eyes and I could hear Daddy he said, "I promise you, I promise you" and then I woke up with Daddy cradlin' me in his arms like I was a baby. I said, "here I am Daddy, was ya callin' me." Daddy was cryin' so hard he couldn't say anything. I said, I'm sorry Daddy, I had to go see Momma and Becky, he just started whaling like I just shot him or somethin'" Jordan embarrassingly tells.

Chapter Nine

Witness

Bang!, a loud gunshot is heard as a rabbit falls in midstride against a bush.

"Ya got 'em Dan!" Carl shouts with glee, "now that was a shot."

"That makes three for me." Dan boasts, "you better add to yer two, cause that ain't gonna make an appetizer for yer Dad."

"Yeah, yeah" Carl remarks, "let's rest I'm tired." as Carl plops himself down on a small boulder.

"Yeah that's a crazy story about yer kid brother, Dan. I bet he saw all kindsa crazy spirits up there. Probably saw the "Snake Dancers" from the Jonka people out west and all the Ghost Dancers." Carl imagines.

"I told ya Carl. The place he went wasn't like that, it was very beautiful and peaceful. All he saw was Mom and Becky, it's like the Christians tell." Dan says.

"Yeah, I've been listenin' to ya for days now talk about that Christian God and stuff, but don't ya still believe our way." Carl asks.

"You know, I've been readin' the scriptures and I've been readin' about 'ndans all over. And to me there's a lotta tribes that have old ways that are a lot like the Christian God's ways. There are tribes that believe in respect to the mountains and trees and animals, and the bible says to respect all God's creatures. Ya don't kill just to kill, there has to be a purpose, like these rabbits."

"Yeah, no mutton tonight, fried rabbit, tastes like chicken." Carl interrupts.

"Many tribes believe in the healin' power of the Creator. The Bible says Jesus healed all the sick, it says He healed them all. Our shaman can't do what Jesus did." Dan preaches.

"Yeah well Jesus didn't turn into a "Skin walker." Carl criticizes, "Besides Jesus is dead and gone. Who's gonna heal the Christians now, smart guy?"

"Jesus isn't dead, stupid, He's still alive, and He'll heal anybody that will really believe in Him, all ya gotta do is trust Him." Dan touts.

"Oh yeah, well I'm not gonna believe it until I see it!" Carl assures. "There's one!" Carl shouts, jumping up with his shotgun, running after the prey.

"There he is right there, over there." he directs as he continues to chase the rabbit.

Carl zigs and zags though the brush chasing the rabbit, then he trips on some sagebrush and tumbles to the ground in a cloud of dust as a loud blast sounds.

"Owwwww!" Carl screams as he continues to tumble and cause dirt to fly into the air. Dan stops his pursuit of the rabbit as Carl screams in agony.

Dan throws down his gun and game and rushes to Carl's aid. He runs up and stands over Carl's ailing body covered in dust.

"Oh my God!" Dan gasps, "Oh my God!"

"Help me!" Carl pleads as he reaches his hand toward Dan.

"Oh Jesus!" Dan cries.

Dropping to his knees next to Carl, Dan begins to take his bare hand and lift Carl's torn jaw back into place.

The blast tore Carl's face in half, entering the bottom of his throat and coming out his cheek, his eye drops without support. Dan tries to hold Carl's face together.

"Oh Carl, Oh Carl, what did ya do?!" Dan moans looking into his friend's face giving up life.

With a whisper of a breath Carl begs, "Help me Dan!."

"Oh my God!" Dan cries, looking around and seeing nothing but desert for miles around.

He rips off his shirt and pushes it against Carl's neck and face, the blood fills the shirt in an instant.

"Oh Carl!" Dan whispers.

"Don't let me die out here Dan, don't let the snakes and coyotes get me!" Carl pleads, "there's … there's corn pollen in my bag, make an offering for me Dan."

Dan puts his head down and slightly shakes it from side to side in pity. He then stops and looks up suddenly with a determined stare.

"Carl, ya don't have ta die here" Dan boldly states, "Remember we were talking about what Jesus can do, just a few minutes ago?"

Carl looks into Dan's eyes and slightly nods, saying, "uhuh."

"Well I said Jesus is alive and will heal anybody that will really believe in Him. Well I believe He can heal ya, you have ta believe too. I know it looks bad buddy, but ya have 'ta believe! Do you believe He can heal ya Carl?"

"Yeah, I believe." he confesses with his last breath, his upper body slumps over to the side giving up life.

"Hold on Carl, hold on buddy!" Dan grits through his teeth.

He holds Carl's head in one hand, his mangled cheek covered with the bloodied tee shirt and the other an image of perfection. Dan grows more concerned, but is filled with greater resolve to prove God.

"Jesus, Carl and I agree and believe in ya together, and we believe you can heal him. Jesus we don't got anybody else. We pray to you, heal my friend. You raised Lazarus from the dead, just like you raised Jordan. Well now Carl needs yer help, like ya helped the blind man and the deaf, and the cripple and the demon possessed and that guy ya put his ear back on. I wasn't there to pray for Mom and Becky, but I believe you would have healed them too, it was for a reason. Please Jesus, heal Carl's face, give him his life back. Save our people. I'll do whatever you ask me, please God, we trust you, we trust you." Dan's prayers stop.

His eyes are still clamped shut. There is deafening silence, as tears stream from Dan's eyes. Dan slowly opens his eyes, batting his eyelashes to have clear sight.

Carl is looking intently into Dan's eyes, he swirls his head in circular motions, he sits up and takes Dan's hands from the blood filled shirt, while Dan looks on in shock and expectation.

Carl's eyes grow less pain filled and more bewildered.

"Take it off!" Carl instructs.

Dan slowly raises his hand back to Carl's face and begins to gingerly remove the shirt. The shirt is drenched in blood.

Dan pries the last of the sticky shirt from Carl's face. Once the shirt is cleared from his vision of Carl's cheek, Dan's face turns from concern to total shock. His face shows expression of astonishment to joy. A smile rises to each cheek.

126

"Oh my God, Carl!" Dan gleefully exclaims, "He did it! He did it!."

Carl's face is clean from the blood and his skin is healed as if there never was an accident at all. Dan turns Carl's chin from side to side.

"It's completely healed, thank you Jesus! Thank you Jesus!" Dan yells.

"Yeah Jesus, thank you, thank you Jesus!" Carl agrees.

Dan helps Carl to his feet and they dance in a circle, stomping up dirt, singing, "Thank you Jesus! Thank you Jesus!"

Five rabbits dash away from the duo.

***

Slam!, as Poncho's hand makes a loud bang on the spool table outside the bar.

"I told ya this squat was gonna happen, now he converted yer boy!" Poncho yells angrily, "Somethin's gotta be done!"

"I told ya he said Jesus glued his face back on!" Jim tells, "My boy wouldn't lie about somethin' like that. He knows how much I hate Jesus and those Christians!"

"Yer boy is a follower, he doesn't know his rear from his melon head!" Poncho growls.

"Hey Darkcloud, that's my boy yer talkin' about!" Jim defends.

"Do you want yer boy and that Morgan kid to convert everybody in town and destroy our Nawhe ways?" Poncho asks.

"Well no, but I'm saying it was a miracle. The boy's face was half blown off and they prayed to Jesus and it was healed. How do ya explain that Poncho?" Jim asks.

"I still don't believe it. It either didn't happen or Conga did the miracle!" Poncho defends. "He probably had pity on the idiot kid, blowin' his face off."

"Well all I know is that squat's being told all over town!" Lenny reports, "Big miracle by Jesus!

Old lady Talltree had those two over there prayin' for her this mornin'. My wife said she's telling that the breast cancer's gone. It's a wildfire I tell ya!"

"Yeah my wife said all kinds of people are stopping by the house for the boy to pray for them. It's outta control!" Jim states.

"We can't wait. We gotta kill the boy!" Poncho says.

"Not my boy!" Jim pipes.

"No not yer boy!" Poncho sarcastically consoles. "Like I said, yer kid's a follower, if we kill the Morgan kid it will die with him. The town will get wise, this is Conga country, not no Jesus state!" Poncho declares.

"Our ancestors have made sure of it a long time before we were here and it's our responsibility to keep our beliefs intact!"

"Alright then we do the kid tomorrow night." Lenny determines.

"I don't know guys, Carl was pretty convincin'" Jim explains.

"Listen big boy, yer either for us or against us, which is it?" Poncho asks.

"Yeah, alright, yer right, tomorrow night. Carl's supposed to meet him at church tomorrow night, but

Carl ain't gonna be going to no church!" Jim sternly informs.

"Sounds like we got us a foolproof plan." Poncho eerily laughs. "Poetic justice, let's do him in the same spot we did his ma and big sister." The trio laughs in evil agreement.

"We'll shred his body in pieces, nobody will recognize him, but they'll know who it is and why he's mutilated!" Poncho salivates.

"Yeah Conga will give us a great blessing!" Lenny imagines aloud.

Chapter Ten

Dueling Dilemmas

A loud screech comes from the little wooden house.

"Yaaaaaaaoowww" screams the older Nawhe man.

Dan kneels beside the man, his hands resting on the bare lower back of the elder. Carl stands with his eyes tightly closed, shaking his head back and forth, his lips constantly move in silent prayer, with his hand tightly gripping the shoulder of the sufferer.

The room is adorned with regalia of skins and antlers, spears and shields hang on the walls. An antique wood burning stove warms coffee as its aroma battles with the scent of Indian fragrances and the musky hides.

Years of newspapers are stacked in the corner, thick dust covers everything including the dingy yellow window panes.

"Oowwwww!" the old man howls, "Oowww, hmmm, oooo, yes, oh yes, gooood." he utters in Nawhe. "That's remarkable my young brothers!" the elder affirms.

"Do you know how long I have felt this agonizing pain, but now, oh now! I haven't felt this good in years." he continues, "You really are spiritual as I have heard, this white man's God has given you a good gift."

"He is real, Gardon." Dan proclaims.

"Yes, He is, I have no doubt." the old man testifies. "My kidneys have been killing me, literally." Gardon tells, "And the dialysis just brings down your whole body and spirit. This sickness haunts me, because of my Nawhe brothers, it's like I told you. They are jealous because I have tried to learn our white brothers' ways for years, and now they try to curse me with this disease.

They know I don't trust them and keep to myself for my own protection. When I heard you two had received great blessings from the white God – Jesus, I called for you right away. I believe the stories you and others have told me about your experiences. And now I have received a great blessing.

Years ago I received a healing in my stomach from Jesus. We used to go to the little white church, my family and I, when I was a young man. We went to the church for food and medicine and clothes, we had to sit in the services for it. But we didn't give our hearts to this Gospel, we just sat there and chanted in our hearts to Conga.

The white preacher didn't know, he would smile at us and we would tell one another in Nawhe, "white fool." But one day I got really sick, I went for medicine, but the white man's medicine didn't work, I became more and more sick.

Finally they sent me to the white man's big hospital in Grants. The doctor there said I had cancer in my stomach and there wasn't anything they could do. Before the winter was over they said I would be dead. It scared me, I was young, I wasn't ready to go to the spirit world. I cried like a newborn, but then I remembered something that white fool said.

He said Jesus is the great physician and can heal any and all sicknesses and disease. The white man's medicine and our Nawhe prayers and medicine wouldn't work. I thought what difference would it make if I was killed by my brothers because I believed Jesus, I was going to die anyway. So I went to the white preacher at night and asked him to pray for Jesus to heal me from this cancer. He did and by the next morning I was healed.

I told my family. My father was bitterly angry with me, but he was my father and would not sacrifice his youngest son. He said "keep this word quiet" so we did. But before too long the village heard what Jesus did and how I believed in Him. Many of the village men came and threatened to kill all of us in our house.

I told my father I would run away and they couldn't hold them responsible for my actions. So we agreed. I was gone for two months, and I kept hearing that preachers words, "if you're ashamed of me before man, I'll be ashamed of you before my Father which is in heaven" it kept eating at me.

I couldn't stand being away from my family so I returned home. It took three days to walk back home. When I got here I found our home burned to the ground with the bodies of my family still here.

I found out the men came back the next night after they agreed to leave my family alone if I left. The same night I left. And they burned our home to the ground with all my family, my father, mother, two brothers, and my little sister. They even went and got my big sister and her husband and baby that didn't live with us and forced them inside before they set fire to them all.

Hatred, ugly, disgusting hatred. Hatred for a God they didn't understand, hatred for their own people that never did them any harm. Hatred for a little innocent baby, my nephew. I promised him I wouldn't ever be ashamed again, by then the preacher left, so I followed Jesus the best I could alone.

Through the years a few Nawhe accepted Jesus and his way. But just like my family they too would pay the ultimate sacrifice. I tried to save some and warn them, but they believed even stronger than I did and they perished in their faith.

I became more and more distant to the tribe. I still walk to the Trading Post for my paper, Old Man Reeves is one of the few people I've talked to in years. I believe in my own traditional way to honor Jesus and Creator.

He doesn't hate us because we are Nawhe, he made us Nawhe. But he didn't make us religious, we did it to ourselves. Religion sets rules to distant those you don't want in.

Creator made us to overcome our fears, He did not give us a spirit of fear, but strength to draw closer to one another and be solid in our walk in harmony with Him and one another. Even though I've been practically by myself most of my adult life, I still love the people, they are my people I have not given up on them. I pray for them every day, and when my friend comes we pray together. I believe Jesus heard our prayers.

I heard about you two, I couldn't believe it, the miracles and those accepting your gifts. I thought I would be dead soon, and look, Jesus healed me again, He's given me a new chance, a new life, a new family!" the old man cries.

Dan and Carl give way to great tears in their eyes. They didn't realize the difference they could have made in someone's life.

Dan snorts and wipes his eyes and blubbers, "We'll be your nephews." The old man falls on his knees, grabbing Dan around the neck and Carl around his knees.

"Thank you Jesus for these faithful nephews." Gardon sobs. "Daniel your great grandfather was the one who stood up for the whiteman's God among our people. Many of the elders and men were against allowing the white church to be built, but Desertwind had a heart for the people and spoke strong words to those against the church. If it hadn't been for your family the Nawhe would have never know the true Creator and His ways."

"I'm not against all our ways, but I know the black journey is a path of darkness, God calls us to a path of light." Daniel continues, "We must come out of our ways that don't build up one another and glorify God."

"When you cross the black journey, you come to the mouth of Donchaseedo. In the white man's language you would say the Canyon of Traditions. This canyon tells the history of our people. From the beginning of time, through many generations of good and hard times. Our people once walked a good path, but their hearts were changed when they began to listen to other spirits. Daniel you are bringing us back to the good path."

The elder continues to teach the two young men for hours in the history of their people, including the beginning.

***

The sky grows dark over the village of Banshee as the sun begins to set. Black clouds begin to engulf the small town as an unsettling atmosphere begins to take claim of the anxious village. The black clouds begin to fall upon the village and snake through the streets as a hungry animal seeking prey. The dwellers of the community sense the spiritual conjuring and become apprehensive to their own existence, not a soul is found outdoors.

As the cloud seeks its objective it nears a tattered shack at the outskirts of the village. The dull thud of a drum and fast shaking of a rattle, as the sound of a venomous rattlesnake comes from the weary structure.

Then as the black cloud tries to penetrate the old house the sound of low moans and chants begin to seep through the wooden slat walls. A gray smoke rises out of the rusted tin stack protruding from the center of the shack's roof.

The cloud begins to rise to the roof of the house and is drawn to chimney as a magnet, snaking along the shingles and up and in the stack. Bam! The drum is struck with a loud beat as the cloud enters the room with the smoke from the fire, causing the room to dim to almost black.

Poncho growls with his chanting, inviting the spirits to enter his home. He holds a drum stick in one hand and rattle in the other. He hits the drum harder and harder, faster and faster, he shakes the rattle quickly as a snake about to strike.

He chants with his lips open wide and his teeth almost clinched. His eyes watch as the cloud circles the room tighter and tighter. It climbs and circles his waist and works its way up his chest and around his neck.

He stops his chanting and opens his mouth as the cloud forces its way in and down his throat. His eyes widen all the more and then begin to tear.

He continues to drum louder and louder and rattle faster and faster. From outside the shack a high pitch scream can be heard as the drumming and rattling stop.

The screaming begins to quiet and then all is silent. Nothing but silence, the cloud has gone.

Then slowly and lowly the drumming begins again, a lone voice is heard singing and then several other voices and drummers can be heard joining in the ominous song inside the shack.

Chapter Eleven

Worlds Collide

"Thank you Dad for letting me go tonight, I'm so nervous about attending this church service." Dan proudly states, "I just wish you and Jordan would go with me."

"Nope, I know a bunch of stuff has been going on here since you became a Christian, stuff I can't argue with. I've seen with my own eyes, but for some reason it's not our time yet to go to church. Can ya understand Dan?" Ben asks.

"Yeah I know, it took me a long time. I know how it is. At least Carl's gonna be there, a couple other new people are gonna be there. Pastor Knows said it's the first he's seen any new attendees in four years." Dan tells, "He's very excited, but not as excited as I am, my first church meetin'!"

"Now I told ya Daniel, you lay low, I hear you and Carl are going around tellin' everybody about Jesus and the miracles he's done. That's good, but don't forget what happened to yer ma and Becky." Ben reminds with great concern across his face. "There's a lotta people in this village that don't like Jesus no matter what. It's been going on for a long time. The elders and people don't understand the Jesus way. For generations they've followed our spiritual ways.

I picked up your Bible and read some real interesting things. These Christian ways are very powerful, very spiritual. I think the people might be changin' a little bit, but there's those that ain't ever gonna change. So you lay low and watch yer back!" Dad instructs.

"I'm not worried, Jesus has my back, He has me and Carl talkin' to a lot of people. He's doin' a lot of miracles with our people. Ms Talltree said Jesus healed her from cancer. Mrs. Thundercloud said her headaches are gone that she had for 20 years. Her grandson was sittin' up eatin fry bread without barfin' like he's been doin' with everything else he's ate in last two weeks.

Old man Reeves' cataracts went away and he said he can see better than when he was a teenager, Gardon swears God is going to do something astounding with us. And what happened to Jordan and Carl, people are very excited, I can't wait to see what He's gonna do next!" Dan reports.

"Alright Danny, yer right. Jesus is really doing some stuff with the Nawhe, but watch out for those three bums. You know who I mean. I think they're the ones who did that to Julie and Becky, so watch out please son." Dad requests. "I don't want to scare ya, but last night there was something going on, and I mean something pretty dark."

"Yeah I know I could feel it. It sent shivers down my spine, but Jesus told me not to be afraid, so I'm not, I'll be careful." Dan agrees. "I think there's some pretty serious evil in the village and like you said. Mr. Darkcloud seems to be a big part of it, is that why you attacked him at the ceremony the other night?"

"Yeah, I've had my suspicions for years, but the tribal cops just wrote it off. They didn't investigate anything, they're Poncho's friends. They didn't even want to come over here from up north, but the state cops said they would come if the Indian cops won't. So they put in their appearance and that was it. Well we can talk more about it when ya get back. Ya better get outta here or yer gonna be late son." Dad prompts.

"OK, I'll tell ya about service later. I love ya Dad."

Dan hurries out the door and briskly walks down the road with his Bible at his side.

Dad stands at the screen door and says in a low voice something he's never told Dan in all his life, "I love you too, son."

Dan's walk across the village this late, somehow reminds him of the black journey before the ceremonies, but he thinks how different this ceremony will be tonight. He can hear music and singing coming from the church as he nears the small little white building.

"We shall wear a robe and crown. Watching, waiting we know not the day when the Lord shall call our soul away, If your fighting, fighting for the right, you shall wear a robe and crown." the congregation of two and Pastor Knows sings as Dan opens the door and steps in.

Daniel is expecting to see many more people, but he's too excited with his first church experience to be too distracted from it.

Pastor Knows immediately sees Dan walk in and motions for him to come on in. Dan walks all the way down to the front pew, stopping to shake the hands of Ms. White Dove and Ms. Bright Cloud standing at their usual spots across the aisle from one another on the second row of pews.

Tears and a smile come from both of the ladies as they stop singing long enough to greet Dan.

"Yer Momma is so proud of you Daniel!" Ms White Dove boasts.

Daniel's eyes glisten with pride and remembrance as he accepts her compliment.

"We've all been prayin for this day." says Ms. Bright Cloud.

Dan grins a humble smile and continues on to front pew. He stands at the front pew, not wanting to miss anything and feeling Jesus is down front and he wants to be there, too.

"How about page forty-four." Pastor Know calls out.

"I have decided to follow Jesus, I have decided to follow Jesus, I have decided to follow Jesus, no turning back, no turning back. Though none go with me still I will follow, though none go with me still I will follow, though none go with me still I will follow, no turning back, no turning back."

Pastor Knows springs from the piano bench and leads the congregation in the last chorus accapela.

"The cross before me the world behind me, the cross before me the world behind me."

As Dan looks up at the tall wooden cross on the wall at the front of the church, he begins to cry and finishes the song with the group.

"The cross before me, the world behind me, no turning back, no turning back."

Pastor Knows motions slowly with his hands for the group to sit down, they seat themselves as slowly as he motioned.

"Thank you folks, what a blessing. When you sing to honor God it draws Him that much closer. Can't you feel how close He is? You can reach out and touch Him. Let's honor him tonight and take up the offering for his house." Pastor requests as he takes a small basket and approaches Daniel, "Pass it back son."

Daniel takes the skimpy basket and looks lost as he wonders what he's to do with it. Ms. Bright Cloud leans forward across Daniels shoulder and places a crinkled up dollar bill in the basket.

Daniel jerks his head in a quick notion and mouths "oh." He reaches in his pocket with his free hand and pulls out a hand of various coins and a pencil and a few pieces of gum.

He sets down the basket on the pew, while he picks through the assortment and places his life savings of ninety-two cents in the basket.

He turns with a humble grin to Ms. White Dove and she gestures with her hand and head that she doesn't have anything. Daniel's eyes turn to pity for her that she hasn't anything for the church.

Pastor Knows approaches Daniel and says, "Thank you son." taking the basket and holding it in both hands with his arms outstretched upwards.

"Thank you Lord for all you bless us with, you have given us so much and we give all we can to help this little church, bless this offering and allow it grow so we can touch this little community again, amen."

"Amen" the trio agree.

"Well, this is a fine night; God has brought us a new creature. The good book says, when we accept

Him He forgives all our sins and places them from us as far as the east is from the west, never to remember them again. And we are now new creatures in Christ. I want to welcome this new creature tonight, Daniel stand back up." Pastor Knows demands.

Daniel humbly rises to his feet. "Daniel, I told you the other day your mother had been praying for this day a long time", as the two ladies agree, "amen".

"All of us promised we would keep prayin' for you and Jordan and Ben. Well the harvest is coming in. One at a time, but they're comin' in. Go ahead and sit down son." as Daniel slowly sits down with a huge grin on his face and lowly motion of his head in agreement.

"Now we were told to expect a few more tonight, and they were coming, but that ol' liar, the devil is at it again. There's word out there tonight that there's gonna be trouble. Well don't you believe it. It's all in God's hands. All we can do is ask Jesus to intervene and watch over us. There are those that were scared off, but let me tell ya something tonight. God is bigger!" the Pastor preaches.

"Amen!" the ladies pipe in harmony.

"God is bigger than any evil. Any obstacle and person of this world. All you gotta do is trust and obey. Jesus said no greater love that a man have than this, that he lay down his life for his friends. He did it. He was the Son of the most high God. Who are we to say, no Lord I won't stand for you. Daniel here did it. I told the boy to take it slow, but in a few days he's had a greater impact on this community than I've had in the 8 years that I've been here. God bless you son. We have nothing to fear, but fear itself. People were scared off tonight, because it's hard to overcome fear. But when you realize what the bible says, that God did not give us fear, but power and love and a sound mind. A sound mind laughs at fear. A sound mind says I'm not going to let it run me. A sound mind says I'm gonna be a Daniel and stand up for my God!

When we lost Daniel's Mom and sister it almost devastated me. I don't know if I could ever go through that again. But let's work while it's day, because night comes when no man can work. I see this young man and my hope is born again for the Nawhe people. I know Jesus is doing something very special through this young man, I even see him taking my place up here some day. Imagine that a Nawhe, pasturing this church for the Nawhe. The Lord says be strong and know that I am God. Now this wasn't my message tonight, but God laid these words on my heart. And any message He gives us is a whole lot greater than any message a man can give you. Be careful tonight going home. Don't be afraid because He walks beside you. Let us stand and pray.

Lord we trust in your word, we believe in you, we know you are with us always, who shall we fear. Lord send your Holy Spirit before each of these and keep them safe and let them know you are with them, Amen." Pastor Knows prays.

After their good-byes, they each turn out into the night in different directions.

As he makes his way home, Dan is so excited to have attended his first service, he can hear the words of the songs still ringing in his heart. He is oblivious to the night, because of the Pastor's message. He knows that Jesus is so real and he wants to tell the world.

He sings, "though none go with me still I will follow, though none go with...."

Suddenly he can hear footsteps rushing along the brush to the side of the road. He quickly glances back and can see several dark figures chasing after him. He has gotten too far from the church for anyone to hear him and his pursuers are between him and the closest homes, he has to run toward home a distant mile.

He tries to dash off but his backward glance throws his stride off and he trips over his own legs. He springs forward, just a few feet from his assailants.

He knows this place, it's the same place of the attack of his mother and sister. He begins to let fear overtake him. About that time he catches the sight of another dark figure to his left side off the road.

It's Shondo. Now Daniel begins to grow afraid, his greatest fear is now in the dark only a few feet from him. Suddenly Dan hears growling near his side, he looks down and sees a huge wolf keep pace by his side.

Dan looks forward almost in a look of it's all over. Then the wolf disappears, but he can still hear the pursuers chasing him.

Then he feels the pain of something crushing against his right knee. He tumbles to the ground. He hits his forehead against the hard dirt road. The pain overcomes his adrenaline.

"Gotcha you squat hole!" a voice grumbles.

Immediately Dan is being beaten with clubs. He tries to protect his body from the blows with his arms and by rolling from side to side, but there are several of them and each blow drains strength from Dan's body.

Dan glances up at his assailants and recognizes all three, "Mr. Douglas!" he calls," please no!"

His best friend's father is caught off guard and stops hitting Dan. He looks down at the battered young man with compassion in his eyes as if it were his own son.

"What are ya doing?" Poncho growls, "finish it!" as he weakens the blows.

Lenny looks at the other two and also stops.

"What are ya guys doing?" he asks.

"Hey we're in this together, kill him!" Poncho directs.

Jim looks eye to eye at Poncho. "I can't, I owe my son's life to him!" he proclaims.

"You coward, he's killin' our ways!" Poncho screams.

"Let them die, it's not worth it!" Jim forcefully growls as he throws his club down, turns around and walks away.

"Get back here, ya coward! Yer gonna answer for this, get back here!" Poncho yells as he kicks Dan.

"What are we gonna do Poncho?" Lenny asks.

"What do ya mean? What are we gonna do, we're gonna kill him, that's what we're gonna do!" Poncho assures.

Poncho raises his club above his head and swings it down upon Dan's head, Dan forehead gushes open, his head spins in dizziness.

Lenny raises his club to join in, when he sees something.

"What's that?" Lenny asks with concern in his voice.

They stop again from their duty of beating Dan.

"What now?!" Poncho asks with disgust.

"Right there! Someone is coming towards us, is that Jim? No, what is that it's a, it's a …run!" Lenny yells, as he runs off into the desert.

"What, what, get back here I don't see nothin'!" Poncho screams, "Get your ass back here! Where are you going, Lenny, get back here!"

Off in the distance is the loud, shrill, blood curdling screams of Lenny.

"That stupid son of a…what is he doin'?" Poncho growls, "Well they may have left, but they left you in good hands, we're not alone out here boy!" as his eyes begin to glow red. "There's no saving you tonight!" as his voice changes to a wicked growl. Poncho's eye sockets begin to sink in like sand.

Daniel can't believe what he is seeing, even though he's seen bazaar events at the ceremonies for years.

Poncho begins to beat Dan again. Dan all the while is trying to protect his body.

He has grown so weak, his life is leaving him, he turns from the fetal position to his back and stares up.

Only he sees the light shining down on him. He sees a figure coming down closer to him and he smiles, "I thought it was time." Dan calmly says.

Poncho is in a frenzy beating Dan. The boy's blood sprays across Poncho's body and face.

Dan hears a voice say, "Be strong. I am with you." He smiles as Poncho finishes his beating.

Chapter Twelve

Fulfillment

The bright sun pierces the white wooden cross sitting on the steeple of the old church. Below in the sanctuary is the sound of loud banging and crashing.

"God didn't call me to kill them, but to save them. It just can't be done, they don't want Jesus. They want the Nawhe spiritual ways! They don't want life for their kids, they want death. They don't want healing, they want suffering and pain!" Pastor Knows shouts as he slams his belongings into boxes.

"Now you know that's a lie and deception of the devil!" Ms. Bright Cloud argues, "Didn't Jesus say himself, Father forgive them for they know not what they do?"

"You're arguing with the wrong one Jennie. I read it, remember?" Pastor Knows fights back.

"Yeah and you should know better!" she counters.

"Look here sister, you're not the one that told Ben his wife and daughter were murdered and see the hate in his eyes for you."

Then two years later had to go tell him, come and get your mangled bloodied son in the street. He's dead too. He was beaten and shredded beyond recognition. If it wasn't for his shirt, I wouldn't have recognized him. They even took his momma's Bible!" the Pastor vehemently states. "I've seen people crushed and devastated before, but that man had the life just sucked out of him.

He grabbed that little boy, the only family he's got left and just about suffocated him with his embrace and tears, he screamed, "NO DANNY!" it would have made the strongest man a bawling baby.

No ma'am , I'm not ever gonna do it again. They can send a pastor who doesn't care, has no feelings. Just preach the gospel, stay out of the street and preach the gospel in these four walls. That's all I ever did and how many did I get killed?" the anguished pastor continues to yell.

"Oh come on now Pastor. You're taking an awful lot of credit." Ms. Bright Cloud defends. "You're right; you stayed in these walls, because the men of this village said not to preach in their streets and homes. Unless you wanted to be buried in the middle of the desert in a grave without a marker. Who could blame ya? But it wasn't you that got those people killed. Every single one of them died for Him!" she points up, "not you.

They made it their own choice, Julie and Becky got killed because the Lord placed on their hearts to start a bible study at their house. Julie knew what she was opening her family up for. Ben finally agreed to let her do it after arguing with her for years about it. Those murderers robbed God, because He was gonna do something special for the Nawhe. You didn't get Daniel killed, he died because God called him. When God calls ya He calls ya. You know ya can't argue with God, Pastor, you of all people know you can't argue with God."

"You know what sister, I'm arguing with Him now and my answer is NO, NO, God the price is too high, no!" Pastor Know proclaims, "I've followed

His plan for years, but I just can't see it any more. Why kill an innocent boy? He was about all I had to look forward to! No! the killing stops here!"

"But Brother, I told ya. I talked with some of the people. They're real mad about what happened to Daniel. They said there's not anything that's gonna stop them from coming." she says.

"Well they can just line up at the cemetery, because that's where they're going to wind up!" Pastor declares, "Here's the keys to the church. They're not going to send you a replacement for a while. You and Sister White Dove do what you can, I pray He watches over you." Pastor Knows states, "I'll see to it the electricity is paid on the church the next couple of months."

Without another word the pastor carries his boxes to an old sedan, loads the trunk, and, with the car packed, he drives quickly away, down the dusty dirt road leading out of town. Ms. BrightCloud collapses on the doorstep staring at the sedan creating a great cloud of dust as it speeds away.

"Lord what are we gonna do now?" she questions, "How hard is it gonna get?"

She looks toward the east and a large flock of ravens begin to pass over the small village, she holds her hand over her mouth and tears stream down her face.

***

The skies are gray and a warm wind blows across the valley as the afternoon ends. Ben and Jordan trudge down the dirt road leading to the community cemetery. Ben mournfully lumbers down the road, mostly grown over with desert grass. He carries a large bouquet of flowers in one hand while holding Jordan's hand with the other as Jordan playfully kicks at rocks along the path.

Ben's face is full of seriousness and disdain. He turns at the gate, swinging the inattentive Jordan, snapping up to his side.

Ben respectfully opens the creaking wooden gate and draws Jordan in close and ahead of him as they enter the humble resting place. They both slowly make their way across the narrow lanes between the graves, reaching the far side of the picketed cemetery.

Ben finds the spot and slowly kneels over the freshly placed wooden cross at the head of his son's grave. His eyes fill with tears as he lowers his head and shakes it from side to side.

"I'm so sorry son. I should have gone with you that night." Ben cries with Jordan at his side.

He then slowly pulls a replica of a commercial airliner from his back pocket and attaches it with wire to the cross.

"I'm sorry Daniel. You never got to fly in that airplane, but I know you're soaring with the eagles now."

Jordan cries, "I love you big brother." kissing his little hand and placing it to the top of the wooden cross. He repeats the process with the other two crosses next to Dan's.

"Love ya Momma, love ya Becky." then he runs across the path and out the gate.

Ben's chins quivers and his eyes fill all the more with broken tears.

"I didn't do too good of a job Julie, with the boys that is, I'm sorry." Ben says fighting back the tears, "Well you got to see both your boys up close in the last couple of weeks. I guess Danny is home with ya now.

I'm so sorry I let ya down, Babe, but I made Jesus a promise the minute He brought Jordan back. I told Him I promise to raise the boys in his church if He brought Jordan back and He did, and I'm keeping my promise.

But I wanted to stop and tell you first, no body's gonna hurt Jordan, I promise you that, I'm not trustin no one with our last treasure!" Ben promises, "He'll be safe."

He picks up the bouquet of flowers he laid by his knees, divides them, cups out dirt with his hand at the base of the small cross and places half the flowers there at his wife's grave and repeats the ritual with the other half of flowers for his daughter.

He cries one more time, "I promise!"

He stands to his feet wipes his eyes and shuffles out of the little cemetery, joining Jordan on the other side of the creaky gate. They join hands again and walk down the road.

The sun is slowly dipping into the western sky as the wind begins to stir. From the view of the little white church Ben and Jordan can be seen in the distance drawing closer to the humble sanctuary.

They walk close enough to hear the sound of beautiful music lofting heavenward from the quaint reservation church. Jordan begins to look up at his father nervously, they approach the entrance of the church when Jordan draws back and breaks his hand free from his father's.

Jordan looks up at his father with terror in his eyes, as Ben turns around to see what the delay is.

"No Daddy, we can't go in there. I don't want to go to the cemetery!" Jordan nervously warns "Everybody that goes in there goes to the cemetery. They forget the Nawhe ways and the spirits get them and they go to the cemetery. I don't want to go in the ground!"

"No Baby, that's not what happened." Ben reasons, "Bad people hurt Mommy, Becky and Dan, but they ... they're not in the ground, they went to a place called heaven. Remember where you saw Momma and Becky in that beautiful place? That's where they are and now Daniel's there with them."

"Then why did we stop at the cemetery? You gave Danny a plane and Momma and Becky flowers?" Jordan argues in tears.

"It's hard to explain Jordy. You just have to understand it's a place to remember those you love. Come on let's go inside, it's starting to get dark." Ben tries to comfort.

Jim jerks open the door and walks onto the little church porch startling Jordan. Jordan screams and runs back down the road. Ben tries to chase after him, but Jim grabs his shoulder.

"No wait Ben." Jim begins, "Let me go after him." Ben looks at Jim with shock and distrust.

"Ben I'm sorry. It wasn't me who done it. I was there, but your boy saved Carl's life and I owe Dan a life, so I give him mine!" Jim professes tearfully. "Carl and I have talked a lot since that night. He told me about Jesus and how he forgives you for any and all the wrongs you ever done. And I believed him and now Ben, because of your boy, I'm a Christian.

Dan gave his life for me so that I could know that Jesus gave his life for me, we were wrong to persecute the Christians. But I can't go on 'til I know that you forgive me too!" Jim says with a broken face filled with remorse.

Ben looks at his son's, wife's and daughter's assailant. His face turns from disgust to sorrow. God's Spirit, cracks through the callous of his heart; and Ben begins to cry again.

"I forgive you Jim. Somehow I know that you weren't the one who hurt them." Ben cries.

Ben turns to chase after Jordan who has disappeared into the dark, but Jim says again.

"Let me go, please Ben, I owe it to his big brother." Jim says.

Ben calmly shakes his head in agreement and Jim runs off into the dark after Jordan.

Jordan runs and runs, tears streaming down his checks, fear pounding in his heart. He looks down the road and sees the nearest house in the far distance, he turns back hoping his father is close behind, but sees no one.

Then suddenly he runs nose to nose with a growling wolf. Jordan screams with horror, the huge wolf mammoths over Jordan, as he screams in desperate horror.

At the church Ben has an uneasiness come over him. He just promised Julie he would protect their last treasure, but now he's entrusted this treasure to a man who was there the night his family was attacked. Ben stares into the black night and cries, "please God bring my baby through this Black Journey."

He glances a nervous smile and enters the church. As the old wooden door creaks to his entrance, he awkwardly looks around the sanctuary to find Ms Bright Cloud leading singing as many of tribe's people are standing singing Christian songs.

The church is filled with a spirit of love, strength and warmth. Faces turn and smile at Ben as he makes his way through the church, several of the newcomers shakes his hand as he goes by.

Ms. White Dove grabs Ben by the arm with tears streaming down her face, her nostrils flare with emotion.

She points down at the front pew and says with a broken voice, "That was Daniel's spot right there."

Ben nods and takes the spot for his own and stands in reverence of his family members who sacrificed their lives so he could be in that very spot.

He listens to words of the many songs and draws comfort from them, all the while anxiously awaiting the arrival of his only son.

The songs end and the congregation sits down, the air is filled with silence, everyone waits for someone to stand behind the podium to give words of wisdom and comfort. Ms. Bright Cloud begins to stand back up.

Just then the church door swings open with a bang. The entire congregation spins around in shock. Many of the new church members retract in their seats. Others have looks of determination as if a great battle is going to be fought.

Ben shoots to his feet ready to wage war for the defense of the church. There in the doorway stands Shondo, with a stern disgusted look on his face.

He stands there for a moment and then moves down the center aisle looking on the face of each person there. Then from behind him appears little Jordan.

He pushes the little boy forward and he runs to his father. Ben shows both relief and concern on his face as Shondo works his way slowly toward the front of the church.

The crowd leans away from the center aisle as if they're ready to make a break for it. Shondo stops parallel to Ben and pulls his lower lip in and nods to Ben.

Ben sits down and continues to watch this invader walk past him toward the pulpit. The old man turns around behind the podium and sternly looks up at the congregation in silence as he narrows his eyes. He looks down and pulls a medicine bag up from his side and places it on the inclined podium.

Gardon looks intently at Shondo, smiles and gestures with his right hand towards his forehead as tipping an imaginary hat.

Shondo slowly pulls out a book with a small silver cross on it. Ben immediately recognizes it as his wife's bible, his son's Bible. The old man opens the pages of the blood stained book and begins to read.

"Blessed are the pure in heart for they shall see God." Ben relaxes in his seat as the rest of the congregation sit up in theirs.

Shondo flips a few pages, "I have told you this so that my joy may be in you and that your joy may be complete. My command is this: Love each other as I have loved you. Greater love has no one than this, that he lay down his life for his friends."

Jordan stands on the edge of the pew peering out the window, oblivious to his father. As the old man begins to preach a message.

"It is God's will to love his children and make a home for them, it our purpose to love one another and love God so they we can one day stand in His holy presence."

Throughout the church the congregation holds onto every word of the former shaman. While on the porch of the little white church lies the huge gray wolf of the old man.

The canine lifts his ears and rises to the seated position, he begins to growl lowly with his mouth closed.

His wary stare looks away from the church. Flickers of small flames circle around the small structure.

The tiny flames begin to grow larger as their bearers slowly draw their torches closer to the church.

Inside Jordan's small calm voice whispers, "Bad people."

"Hush Jordan." Ben whispers.

Poncho approaches the front of the church, calling out, "Burn it down! kill them all!"

Back at the pulpit Shondo stops speaking and looks around as in a heighten state of spiritual warfare.

"Great Spirit!" he calls, "Protect these your children!"

From the sky high above the church the many attackers can be observed drifting toward the church. Then suddenly, in the silence of the night a groaning moan can be heard high above the church, a howling of a great rushing wind approaches. A blast of the powerful wind strikes the torch bearers and blows out the flames and flips the attackers in mid air.

The crowd begins to struggle to their feet; they dash off in every direction away from the church.

"Conga!" several yell.

As Poncho sees the attack fail he screams, "NO! Kill Them! Kill Them!"

The wolf on the porch rises and begins to growl louder in Poncho's direction.

Poncho attempts to re-light his torch, when he hears the sound of a loud cat screeching behind him. He turns around and peers into the darkness with great fear.

His eyes grow wild and dart from side to side. His shirt begins to ripple and his upper chest to his neck starts to bubble and swell.

The sound of a large mountain lion screams within feet of the terrified maniac.

He raises his torch to strike at the intruder as an enormous black panther plunges at his face, knocking him to the ground.

Poncho screams, "NO!" as the panther slams his claw into his neck and chest ripping a large slash into his flesh.

The wound bursts open as a wild black cloud is forced out the opening.

Poncho shouts "NOoooo!" as the panther rips the man to pieces.

The screams can be heard from the porch of the church as the wolf lies back down.

In the distance above the town a curtain slowly closes at Shondo's little cabin.

Chapter Thirteen

Astonishment

A black night in the late evening reveals a tattered small house with dimly lit windows, the muffled sound of cartoon characters can be heard coming from the structure.

Quickly a dark figure dashes from behind a bush and darts toward the small framed house.

Inside the house we rotate around a worn cloth recliner, where a young boy sits attentively watching his cartoons. He smiles with his mouth and eyes and he enjoys the cartoon characters display slap stick comedy.

The dark figure circles around behind the house quickly moving from window to window. Finally the figure finds a spot where he can view the child through a torn piece of curtain.

His eyes can be seen intently staring at the small child.

From inside the house the child begins to turn his head from side to side as if something is out of place.

The intruder lowers his head below the window sill. Jordan shakes off the feeling and once again becomes engulfed in his television.

The dark figure pulls out a large knife and slowly places it below the window and begins to pry it open.

Jordan can hear the scratching at the window and sits up and begins to look around the room apprehensively. Jordan's head stops wandering the room and he realizes the noise is coming from the window.

He looks intently at the window. Suddenly the window pops open with a screech startling the boy, he screams in fright as the wind blows the curtain open. Jordan jumps from the chair and runs screaming down the hallway into his bedroom.

"Daddy, Daddy!" the youngster screams in the empty house. The boy slams his bedroom door closed and dives under his half made-up bed.

The terrified child can hear what sounds like moans coming from outside. The front door knob begins to slowly turn, and the door is pushed open.

The boy peering from beneath his bed can hear the front door creak open and footsteps rhythmically walk across the wooden living room floor and down the hall toward his bedroom door.

The child's eyes widen with fear and anticipation as his jaws tighten with a large swallow, his face practically trembling with agony.

The door knob turns slowly as the child intently stares in fear. The door finally begins to open with an eerie creak as a haunted house.

As the door is shoved open the last few inches the boy jumps back in fright beneath the bed.

"Jordan?" a stern calm voice calls.

"Daddy?" Jordan calls back surprisingly.

"Boy what are ya doing under that bed?" Ben questions. Jordan crawls out from his hiding place.

"D...Daddy there was someone at the window! He tried to break in. I could see him coming through the window!" Jordan accounts.

"Yeah, I saw someone up against the house. I hollered at him and he took off running like a rabbit. There was no way I was gonna catch him." Dad informs.

"Ya saw him Daddy?" Jordan asks.

"Yeah, I first saw the flash of his knife by the moonlight." Dad adds.

"He...he had a knife Daddy?" Jordan's fear returns.

"Aw don't worry about it Jordan, it was probably some kid playing around. I'm sorry I left ya here by yourself.

Next time I tell ya come on and go to the trading post with me, don't tell me about no cartoons." Ben instructs.

"Yer not gonna get no arguments from me Daddy." Jordan agrees.

Ben smiles, "Well, I'm glad to hear that, come on boy. I got some fried chicken from the tradin' post, let's eat."

"Mmmm, fried chicken, it tastes like chicken." Jordan proclaims.

"Whatya mean? It is chicken!" Ben argues.

"Dan always said "the tradin' post chicken tastes like chicken." Jordan comes back.

"What? He was just joking with ya." Dad informs.

As they continue to bicker back and forth, the dark figure peers through the window at the pair.

A sack of flour slams on the wooden counter.

"Yeah, that's the third time somebody was up against the house looking through the windows." Ben tells, "Ms. Darkcloud said she saw somebody a week ago, he ran off when she turned on her light and two weeks ago I heard some dogs barking and looked out and saw him, but this is the first time he tried to get in the house."

"Ya better get cha a gun. Ya think they're comin' back?" Jim asks.

"Ya know we hadn't seen 'em for six months. Since that night at the church. I don't think they'd try that stuff again." Ben states.

"I don't know Ben, I've been hearing talk that someone is out stalking in the night. I didn't want to say anything like a scary cat, but last week Carl came screaming outta his room. He said that someone was tapping on his window. We ran outside to see some guy running off across the open field. There was no catching him he was quick. If he's got some buddies there's no telling what they'll do." Jim tells.

"Ms. Sims said she saw somebody looking in the windows during church service last Sunday night."

"Well, I tell ya what when he comes back, I'll be ready for him." Ben proclaims.

Again the night is black around the small house, and the sound of laughter comes from within as Ben and Jordan are enjoying a comedy show.

And again the stealth black figure comes out of the brush and presses himself against the windows of the house.

His eyes peer through the torn curtain once more, but this time the window is open, causing the curtain to gently sway with the cool breeze of the wind.

The intruder reaches his dark hand into the window and grasps the curtain; he pulls it open enough to reveal the duo laughing and enjoying their show.

The eyes of the onlooker narrow as his jaw begins to lightly quiver. Soon the intruders eyes begin to glisten at the scene of the happy pair.

Behind the stalker on the ground the light contours of a face can be seen. Two eyes pop open shedding aside the sand.

The eyes in the ground fix on the back of the dark figure. Then another set of eyes in the sand also pop open.

The two sand men rise out of the dirt as a warm mist rising from a pond. The eyes of the intruder turn from the pair inside and shift to the side and downward in knowledge of the presence of the sandmen.

Suddenly the three struggle and screams and yells are heard as Jordan jumps into his father's lap.

"Grab him!" a voice calls. The sound of thuds are heard as punches are thrown.

"Aarrrg!"

"Look out!"

"Don't let'em go!" is yelled from the fight of the trio.

"Bring him around front!" Ben yells, as he rushes from the open window to the front door.

Jordan stands terrified alone in the living room as his Dad rushes out the front door.

Ben joins the scuffle.

"Bring him into the light!" Ben orders. Ben and the others all burst through the door opening, grasping the intruder.

"Now let's see who we got here." Ben steps back while Jim and Carl each hold an arm of the struggling intruder.

The father and son team tighten their grips on their captive until he realizes he can't do anything and stops his struggling.

The head of the intruder slowly rises. Ben's eyes open in shock. All is silent in the room.

Little Jordan breaks the silence. "Danny?" Jordan says in a quiet questioning voice.

Ben looks at the intruder with broken, concerned eyes shaking his head in disagreement.

"No you're not Danny!" Ben whispers, "We buried my son he's dead!" Ben tearfully continues to whisper.

Jim and Carl loosen their grips and step from behind him to face him from slightly in the front on each side of the boy, looking intently at his face.

"It's me Daddy! I'm not dead!" Danny whispers tearfully, shaking his head slowly from side to side. Jordan grabs his father's leg, no one still believing its Dan.

"They killed my boy! I identified his remains. He was so badly beaten. All I could recognize was his clothes." Ben relays in short, tight-lipped sentences.

"It wasn't me Daddy. It was Lenny." Dan says.

"What! No! My son wouldn't have run away from his family all this time letting us think he was dead!" Ben cries through gritted teeth.

"It was Shondo. Shondo saved me. They beat me to the point of death, I saw Jesus!" Dan cries, "He was so beautiful, the light was so beautiful. He told me it wasn't my time yet."

Jordan can no longer contain himself, "Danny!" he yells as he jumps into his brother's arms.

The two boys embrace with powerful hugs and tears. Ben joins in the hug and tear fest.

Carl embraces his friend with tears in his eyes and Jim finally bear hugs the whole bunch, with a emasculated show of emotion.

"I've missed you guys, but I can't breathe!" Dan gasps.

They all inch away from the boy as Ben asks, "Where have you been and what did Shondo have to do with all of this?"

Dan begins to recount that faithful night.

"I was walking home that night from the church service. I was so excited, the songs just lifted me and God's presence was overwhelming. I was trying to sing one of the songs, it just kept lifting my spirit. Then I could hear somebody chasing me, I was afraid of those three doing something to me."

Jim's head lowers.

"They were getting close. I looked back and then I tripped. I got back up as quick as I could and ran as hard and fast as I could.

Then I heard someone on the side of the road I looked over and it was Shondo. Well right then and there I knew I was dead.

I ran a couple more strides and I could hear something growling right next to my side. I look down and saw this huge grey wolf running with me. I knew it was Shondo, and I got so scared I was ready to give up. Then the wolf disappeared.

But I could still hear someone chasing me they were so close to my back. I recognized the place. It was where Momma and Becky got killed. I knew it was over, and just about then something hit me in the knee and down I went.

I hit the road so hard it hurt so badly and then they started beating me with clubs. It was just like the night of the ceremony when they beat us, it hurt so badly, every time they hit me I could feel more and more strength leaving me.

Finally I saw that one of them was Mr. Douglas, and I said "Mr. Douglas, No." And he stopped hitting me."

"I'm so sorry Daniel!" Jim cries, as Ben looks at him with disgust.

"No, Mr. Douglas. If it was just the other two I would be dead now." Dan justifies. "When you stopped the others did too and you walked away. The other two started beating me again until the wolf came back. Lenny seen the wolf and took off running. Poncho kept beating me. He finally hit me in the head, that's when I saw Jesus. It was like in the Bible when Stephen was being stoned to death, but then he looks up and sees Jesus. I saw this beautiful bright light beaming down on me; I don't think Poncho could see it. But I saw Jesus and he said in an incredibly peaceful voice it wasn't my time that he had much more for me to do."

So I just had a peace and closed my eyes and went to sleep. I found out later that Poncho walked off he thought I was dead, Shondo came and picked me up and carried me to his house.

It was his wolf that chased Lenny away. The wolf chased him back to the spot where I was laying and he tore him to shreds. Shondo took my clothes back and put them on Lenny, so everyone who was after me would think that I was dead."

I was unconscious for several days. It took months for all of my broken bones to heal. Shondo didn't want me to come home until he knew I was gonna make it. There wasn't any sense in everybody going through two funerals for me. I've been coming around the last couple of weeks. I wanted to see you and Jordan. Shondo said it wasn't safe, but I told him I had to."

Ben says, "I understand son, but don't worry, your enemies are gone." As they hug and cry again.

The men visit for hours over the details of the lost months recounting the events leading up to that faithful night.

About the Author

Raymond Davilla is Founder and President of Native Christian Way and Executive Director of Native Way Media. Raymond is of the Wichita and Affiliated Tribes of Oklahoma, he grew up among his people in the small native community of Anadarko, Oklahoma. Raymond was exposed to a multi-cultured background among many native tribes both as a youth and as an adult. The most enjoyable times he recalls growing up, were the powwows across Oklahoma. People gathered from every tribe around and shared their culture of various native dance, food and traditions. The color and pageantry of the graceful and traditional dancers always drew Raymond's interest to a heightened state of respect and awe.

Raymond is overwhelmed even today by the memories of stories told by elders, sharing the past regarding; religion, history and good times. Native people hold a common bond of respect toward the elders, because this leads the way to a successful future while honoring a trying past.

As Raymond entered his adult years after leaving college at the University of Oklahoma, he discovered a new walk with a Creator that his people always followed. It was in a neighboring town that he discovered Jesus Christ as Savior and Lord. God had many things in store for this soon to be minister that would lead him around the country for God's honor. The Lord led Raymond in a power spiritual walk in a place among his white brothers.

Raymond would serve as youth pastor, singles' pastor, associate pastor and senior pastor with various churches both native and white across several states. The experience in these positions has proven to be priceless at each new church adventure. Raymond pastored in conventional, contemporary and the contextual churches.

In 2007, Raymond produced and hosted a local 30 minute television program on Christian television. "Spirit Walkers" was a talk show format program that focused on Native American issues, as well as educated the non Native on Native American culture. The program hosted a variety of guests from Grammy winner Tom Bee, to local ministers and Native cultural leaders. The program had a potential viewing audience of 900,000, covering most of the state of New Mexico.

Raymond has written a script for a full feature film, Black Journey, as well a novel manuscript of the same name. This project is part of a trilogy currently in development.

In addition, Raymond has developed and hosted various promotional and training videos for his non profit organization.

Are you a Native American author?

Do you have a story about Native American culture?

Would you like to see your book published by a Native American owned publisher?

 Then you need to visit our website
www.spiritwalkerpress.com

We are accepting submissions for:
- Fiction
- Nonfiction
- Biographies
- All stories must be authored by Native Americans or about Native America

For submission information, please visit our website.

www.spiritwalkerpress.com

Breinigsville, PA USA
31 March 2011
258875BV00001B/5/P